She's Still Here

By

MISTY L. SHEPHERD

To Kaylee Victoria Sidney, Allison Summer, Patrick Matthew, and Noah Luke, you make my world go round. Your brave and kind souls are everything and more that I ever wanted and prayed for. To Willow Ann and Baby McKinney, you're the most wonderful little things that bring immense joy to my life and complete me. To Andrew and Kayla, the people God hand-picked for my children to love and share their lives with, thank you for loving them so dearly and for loving me too. To my husband, Patrick, your magical heart is my favorite thing, and I never want to live without it.

Contents

Prologue

"Liam…the kids are gone." Ivy knew her mouth was moving; her dry tongue and cracked lips were forming words. But they were falling almost silent. The sound that expelled from her was merely a whisper. Her body was intact, but her soul wasn't. It wasn't the small amount of physical red blood spilling from her exterior wounds, but inside, she was dying like a wounded animal lying in the darkness on the road alone and in pain.

"Ivy…" Liam's cheeks turned red after one word in one millisecond, and his skin felt like fire all over his body. He stood to his feet. He needed to sprint to the mother of his children. "What do you mean, "gone" Ivy?" his heartbeat pulsated in his fingertips while tightly gripping the phone. His eyes closed as he silently prayed that it wasn't the kind of "gone" that meant he could do nothing to get them back. He begged God that the last time he held Kimber in his arms as she drank from her star-covered sippy cup full of apple juice wasn't the last time he'd look into her eyes. Just one day ago, he held Ben's little hand in his as they walked into daycare, both trying not to cry, as they knew their time together had ended until the next weekend. That couldn't be the last time Liam breathed him in, savoring the smell of Cheerios and a little dirt he had stopped to play in as they were getting in the car that morning. It just couldn't be the last time. Liam could hear Ivy trying. She was trying to speak, trying to tell him.

"Where are you, Ivy?! I'm coming to you! Right now!" Liam was already running and searching his pockets for the truck keys.

"I'm at Riverside Park." Ivy's voice trembled, but Liam understood her loud and clear. Especially the word *river.* He imagined the murky brown water rapidly flowing over the sharp rocks from all the rain, full of debris, high up on the bank.

"I'm on my way."

"Liam, baby, please hurry. We need you." It was the last thing he heard her say to him before the line fell silent. It was also the last thing he expected her to call him. She hadn't referred to him as "baby" in what felt like a lifetime. He suddenly felt responsible for whatever tragic thing is taking place at Riverside Park. He wasn't there, and he should have been.

Chapter One

NOW

For some strange reason, Ivy had expected chaos. She expected a courtroom full of men and women in black business attire, scurrying around with beads of sweat on their foreheads. She expected the wooden pews to be full of people, shoulder to shoulder. What people? She didn't know—just people. Maybe Hugo's mom, she only smiled at Liam when they used to drop the kids off at daycare together. Ivy felt the redhead's burning attraction for her husband and the father of their children every time. Yes, Ivy thought; I assumed she would be here. Or maybe Liam's entire family. They never traveled here to visit during the holidays or special occasions, but Ivy would have guessed that they would have driven for days to be present for this. However, none of those things are what is happening today.

Instead, Ivy sits in a small room at a wooden table two doors down from the actual courtroom. There aren't any windows. No décor boasts on the four bare walls. It's cold, much like Ivy's body right now. She's so cold that she's numb; this way, she feels no pain. The attorney she hired sits nearby with her long bare legs crossed as she scrolls through her phone. It's quiet. There's no chatter nor banging from a judge's gavel. Ivy nervously turns her gold diamond wedding set around and around on her finger slowly. She knew today would hurt. Just not this badly. "Be numb." She reminded herself.

The heavy door opened abruptly. The air changed; the lighting changed. Ivy's breathing changed. A tall, thin man with subtle cologne, holding a briefcase in one hand and a cell phone in the other, walked in and immediately rounded the table to find his designated seat across from Ivy's attorney.

Then there he was. The next to enter the room was Ivy's husband. His entrance was calmer, slower, and less anxious to be there. Those eyes. Those beautiful blue eyes. Kind eyes. Ivy tried to look away. She also tried to remind herself to keep breathing, to keep it together, and to stay numb. But she was failing. He took her breath away the same way now as he did then. The only difference was that it used to be because she loved him so much; now, even though she still loves him, it's because she has lost him. He's no longer hers. And she is no longer his. Not after today. Not for a while now, really.

"Hello, Mrs. Cameron; I'm Jake. It's nice to meet you finally." Liam's attorney extended his hand. Ivy took it and offered half of a smile and a tender nod.

Liam sat next to his attorney as he unbuttoned his suit jacket. He couldn't help but look at her. Jake had just referred to her as "Mrs. Cameron". She had beared his last name for so long now it was strange to think of her as being called by her maiden name or, worse, another man's last name. He couldn't stand the thought of it. Rage mixed with regret and sadness rose from the depths of his soul to his throat and choked him. He suddenly felt how small the room was. And still, he's trying not to look at her. Her gaze meets his, and he notices the pain in her eyes. He sees her stiffened shoulders, her lips taut, and she's trying her best not to look at him.

"Mr. Cameron, I have a list of items my client requests to remain in her possession. Please review the list and check the ones that you would like to discuss." Ivy's lawyer hurriedly pushed the paperwork across the table.

"Of course." Liam nervously took the white piece of paper. As he silently read all the items listed from number one to one hundred and twenty-three, he could imagine where each item was in their home. For example, item number nine lists the name of their golden retriever, Holden. They drove three hours away to pick up the little guy. Ivy had spent weeks, maybe longer, trying to find the right dog for their family. Liam was reluctant, not excited. He felt spread thin with work, kids, and the house and thought a dog would be chaotic, except he wasn't. Holden was like a third child. He quickly belonged. Maybe from the first look even. Much like the first time he ever saw Ivy. He just knew. You just know when something or someone belongs with you. He misses Holden lying over his feet in bed at night, even though it had been challenging to get comfortable. He misses their understanding when Holden wanted something, whether it was a drink of water, to go outside, or just to be loved. Those things were all one of the same, really. But, as much as Liam loves and misses Holden, he would never take him away from Ivy and the kids. He and Holden already had an understanding about that too.

He continued skimming over the rest. As he moved past listed items like cars and furniture, he got to the tough part. It was the things Ivy didn't want. The items that weren't on the list. He didn't want them either. He couldn't see them every day. For instance, she had not listed their boat. He still remembers the first time they took it out on the lake. The weather was perfect, and it was a Monday, which meant the water was calm, and they were practically the only ones creating a wake. They left the kids with the sitter because they needed to learn to launch the boat from the ramp and attempt to park the brand new black and white, twenty-four-foot cabin cruiser into her slip for the first time. Liam still remembers how the warm sun kissed Ivy's skin that day. He remembers how her long dark hair refused to behave and stay tucked beneath the hat she took from the dash of his truck that morning. The boat was beautiful, but his wife was breathtaking, much like Ivy still is today. He missed the white one-piece that she wore on the lake that day. He missed everything about that day.

"You don't want the boat, Ivy?" His tone appeared firm, more so than he intended it to.

Ivy's heart imploded. Mostly because of the sound of his voice. But also because she knew that the boat would be sold. She cleared her throat, "No, I don't want the boat, Liam."

Mrs. Knowles interrupted. "Mrs. Cameron wishes to sell the boat, and then the money can be equally divided between you. I understand that my client's friend, Mr. Joseph Pratt, would like to purchase the boat if you agree that…"

"No damn way. That's not happening." Liam's tone was as firm and stern as he intended this time. His attention shifted focus from Mrs. Knowles to Ivy. She was looking down. "Ivy, he's not getting our boat." He said it as straightforwardly and as behaved as possible. There were other words, other things he'd like to say, but that would be inappropriate, much like it was inappropriate to suggest something as insane as the new man in his wife's life would even step foot on that boat. He couldn't think of Joseph untying the rope from the dock, removing the bumpers and placing them under the seats, and then holding Ivy's hand as he drove. Absolutely not.

"That's fine; we are okay with the cabin cruiser "Dance with Me" being sold in the estate sale rather than a private sale. Moving on." Mrs. Knowles quickly scribbled on one of the papers in her folder and then began talking about something probably important, but Liam was fading. His ears were ringing. How could he have messed up this badly? He gave it all away; his dog, boat, kids…his wife. Essentially, he handed over his whole life to another man. He knew he had little to say in almost everything at this point. Joseph could watch cartoons with Kimber on a lazy Sunday afternoon and laugh. He could play kickball with Ben in the yard after school. He can even lay in their bed next to his wife… but the one thing Liam can stop Joseph from laying a finger on is their boat. And if this is all he's got, he'll take it.

Ivy could feel Liam's thoughts. She could smell his jealousy. She could taste his angst. She hoped that he couldn't tell that she was about to break. She hoped she appeared strong, independent, healed, and in love with another man. None of those were true, but she hoped he thought they were.

After nearly an hour of mediation, the meeting was coming to a close. And just like that, it was over. Or was it?

The final paper requiring two signatures was laid on the table for both Liam and Ivy to read and sign.

The words "Dissolution of Marriage" were in bold print. They must have read them in unison because both of their heads shot up to look at one another simultaneously, pens in hand.

Liam wanted to beg. He wanted to get down on both knees, take her hands in his, and beg her. Beg her for forgiveness, a new beginning, and for her to love him no matter what, like she promised to do when they said their vows. However, he knew he would be held accountable for his broken promises. The broken promises that brought them here. Besides, he had already begged—more than once. And still, they are here today, ending their marriage.

Maybe, he could ask one more time. Perhaps his wife would surprise him, and her answer would be different than before. But he refrained. It was too late. He knew it, and now it was time to accept it.

Ivy couldn't hear the attorneys over the sound of her heart beating in her ears. She waited for Liam to say something. Anything. Everything he's already said. But he didn't. He just sat there. He was looking back at her, staring into her eyes. Her insides were melting; whatever superpowers were helping her stay numb earlier were wearing off. Quickly. She couldn't do this anymore. The time had come. Ivy pulled the paper close, signed her name, stood to her feet, picked her purse up off the floor, and left. She could still feel his eyes on her as she walked out the door, but she didn't look back, hesitate, or stop. She couldn't. She couldn't let him see her cry.

Much like their marriage, Liam watched as Ivy ran away, and he remained behind. He froze. Liam didn't know why he was shocked that she signed, but he was. He followed suit and signed the paper. The attorneys gathered their things, then empathetically excused themselves. Liam still couldn't move. He needed a minute. He just lost his wife. It was okay not to be able to move, not to be able to breathe, to drown in a sea of regret. The damage was done, and there was no taking any of it back. He no longer had a wife and was trying to stay above the tide that was pulling him under.

Chapter Two

THEN

"Dance with me?" Ivy heard his sweet voice before she laid eyes upon his handsome face. He whispered in her ear from behind as she sat with some girlfriends at a table ordering more drinks.

Liam watched as she turned to face him; her cheeks flushed from the alcohol. Her smile was wide but shy. "Excuse me?" She asked from the rooftop bar in Charlotte, North Carolina, on a warm summer night under the stars.

"Will you dance with me, please?" He held his hand out to help her from her seat.

His blue eyes were mesmerizing. Suddenly Ivy worried that she had drunk too much. Was this man real? Ivy looked around at the different groups of people lingering at one table or another. Music played quietly over the speakers. So quiet that it was difficult to hear the words. She noticed that no one was dancing. She wasn't even sure that people were supposed to dance.

"I'm sorry, but I don't think they have dancing here." She moved close to his face and whispered back to him. She could smell his aftershave. He smelled like clean soap and bourbon, and she liked it.

"Come with me." He whispered and then winked.

Ivy didn't resist. She couldn't. She was already under his spell. He was like magic. He took her hand into his, then led her to the corner of the roof, but not so far away that the music faded completely. They danced beneath strings of warm lights and the stars in the sky. God made one thing, and man made the other, yet both shed light on something new and rare.

Liam pulled her close. She felt his body heat, making her own temperature rise. "I'm Liam."

Ivy let his name bounce off her heart and then come back. She knew at that very moment that his name would be burned into her soul until she took her last breath. She just knew.

"My name is Ivy." They didn't have to whisper but chose to anyway.

"Hi, Ivy."

"Hi, Liam."

Both smiled at one another. His was wide and bright; hers was shy and afraid. Afraid of the kind of big moment this was. Her mama always told her that she would know when it came to her soul mate. She had always considered the statement to be cliché and untrue. Impossible even. But this man was proving her wrong.

While everyone else mingled, drank, and had dinner, Ivy and Liam held onto one another, swaying to the sound of their own laughter. And they remained there long after the others left, the tables were cleared, and the strings of lights went dark. They only needed the stars and one another.

It wasn't until the rain began to fall that Liam grabbed his jacket to cover Ivy so that she didn't get wet, and they bolted for the door, only to find it was locked. They were stuck on the roof all night in the dark. They realized this immediately. They didn't panic or reach for their phones to call for help. Ivy lowered the soaking wet grey sports jacket, allowing the raindrops to fall around her.

Liam couldn't refrain. He ran his thumb over her wet lower lip, asking her with his eyes if he could kiss her. He didn't need to ask because she tip-toed and kissed him first. She couldn't wait any longer. She needed to know what forever tastes like.

Chapter Three

NOW

"Are you okay?"

It was the last voice he wanted to hear right now. It still felt wrong after all this time. Especially today.

"I'm good." He lied. And she knew he did.

"I don't know what to say." Scarlett's heart skipped a beat.

"I don't want you to say anything." Liam rested his head on the back of his truck seat. It was dark in the courthouse parking garage. He felt exhausted, and his bones ached. That's what a broken heart will do to you. It will break your bones.

"Can I see you?" Scarlett's voice was low, afraid to say something wrong or anything that would make him run away again.

He should say no like he should've a year ago. But he didn't. He would run to her, like always.

And like always, Scarlett would know he was in her arms but wishing he was in his wife's. She could sense his regret and hoped that it would fade with time. She would wait forever if she had to. After all, Ivy's no longer his wife. She would take more of him now. More than he realized he was giving away.

Meanwhile, Ivy walked. She walked out of that room, out of the courthouse, and onto the streets. She didn't pay mind to her heels. Or the buzzing from the phone at the bottom of her purse.

She just walked. When she got to Tia's front door, she only needed to knock once before the door opened. Her best friend stood with open arms, welcoming her to come inside, where she let her ugly cry for as long as she needed to.

"I felt so stupid. It felt like my divorce was bigger than what it was today, Tia. It was one small room, two attorneys, Liam and me. That's it. It was so much more than that, you know? I expected more, like a big shebang. And it just wasn't. It was sad."

"How was Liam?" The five-foot-six woman with long, curly blonde hair laid her hand upon Ivy's. "I mean, did he agree to everything?"

"He was sad. He looked tired. He refused to allow Joseph to buy the boat. I knew that would happen; I just didn't expect him to get so upset about it."

"He got upset?" Tia handed her a cup of hot coffee with sweet cream and watched Ivy take a sip and close her eyes with pleasure.

"He did. Very jealous, which complicates things. I need that money."

"I already told you if you need money, all you have to do is say so."

"That's kind, Tia, but no. I couldn't pay you back. Besides, I start my new job next week. Things will get easier then." Ivy knew this was true; money wouldn't be as tight once she started teaching third grade. But it would be much more challenging to manage Kimber and Ben. But she knew it would work out; she just needed to find ways to make it work. "Besides, you need to save for your big move." Ivy gave a little nudge and smiled at her friend sitting beside her on the sofa.

"I can't believe I'm leaving. It feels surreal. I'm going to miss you. We will stay in touch. Everyday. I promise."

"I know, I just hate it. I hope Kyle knows what a prize he's won."

"Kyle knows it; the one I'm worried about it is my mom. With her having cancer, it makes this new move bittersweet. She sometimes takes more than I can give, you know?" Tia didn't allow the tears swelling in her eyes to fall. She swiped them away before they could.

"Your mom and Kyle have won the lottery. I wish I could keep you." Ivy returned the gesture by laying her hand over Tia's. "We haven't been friends long, but it feels like you're the piece that has always been missing from my life. You've gotten me through the hardest thing I've ever gone through. I owe you so much. I'm going to miss you." Ivy didn't forbid her tears to escape and stream down her face. This past year, she learned through her divorce that when you feel something, you feel it. You don't push it away. You fight for yourself and the people you love. You tell them that you love them. You tell them that you hate them. Except for earlier today, today she needed to be numb; she was stronger that way. And she needed to be strong to finalize her divorce from Liam.

"You owe me nothing except those adorable kids." Tia joked and squeezed her friend.

"I still love him, you know?" Ivy had to catch her breath; something invisible and silent kicked her in the gut after she said the words aloud. "After everything, after all the disappointment, all the embarrassment...after her, I still love him."

"Don't do that, Ivy. Stay strong. It's over. Let him go." Tia's voice was stern and rigid. Ivy's insides were hollow. It terrified her that she might always be just that... hollow.

Chapter Four

THEN

"You can do this, baby; I'm so proud of you." Liam knelt beside Ivy as she lay in the hospital bed, kissing her sweaty forehead and holding her hand. He was in awe of her bravery, and she was in awe that they were bringing a baby into this world together. Her eyes locked with his. It's rare to catch a glimpse of this type of love, an extraordinary and rare thing that can easily be missed. The moment you look into the eyes of the person who just made you a mother or a father.

Everything faded. The nurse hands the doctor everything he needs; the other nurse records the time, Ivy's vitals, and the baby's heart rate. The doctor tells Ivy when to push and when to stop. It was just the two of them. Ivy cried out from her core and used every ounce of strength she had and didn't have. Finally, after one last push, they were a family of three.

They had a son. Benjamin Cole. Liam instantly could tell he had his eyes and his mother's lips. It was indescribable. "He's perfect, Ivy. Perfect."

As soon as the nurse let Liam cut the cord, they placed the baby on Ivy's chest. Like true animal instincts, once mom's skin touched baby's skin, her arms enclosed around him, Benjamin nestled to her on the outside just as he had on the inside for so long. Liam's arms stretched over his wife and child, loving and protecting them. Now and always.

They expected to feel full, proud, and tired when Ivy delivered their child, but they never expected what would happen once they went home and once family and friends had come and gone.

She felt it even before Ivy opened her eyes on their third day home after leaving the hospital. It was something strange, something unwelcome, something wrong. She first noticed the sun seemed to shine through the bedroom curtains a little duller. And then, after Liam placed their son to her breast, she felt trapped and anxious. The feeding was long and painful; no matter what she did, Benjamin appeared uncomfortable and hungry, but not for her.

Afterward, Ivy practically sprinted to the bathroom. She couldn't wait to have a few minutes to herself. She needed to close the door and lock it. But disappointment set in as soon as she stepped beneath the hot water. She found no solace, comfort, or familiarity when she touched the vanillafragranced body wash to her wet skin. Instead of savoring this time to herself, she wanted to hurry. She needed to get back to the baby. She needed to see Liam, and she needed to load the dishwasher. These feelings continued throughout the rest of the day. She couldn't help but count the minutes until she could slide into bed beside her husband in the darkness and just be. She needed quiet. And yet, when the lights were turned off, and her husband slept beside her, she felt insanely sad and alone. She felt afraid. Then she felt angry that she was being weak. Nothing felt the same. Not their home, not her own body, not family, and not even Liam lying in their bed beside her. She was exhausted but not too tired to cry. She cried into her pillow, a gut-wrenching, helpless cry for no one to hear. Especially Liam.

Unsuccessful at being quiet as a mouse. Liam woke. He rolled over in their bed and pulled her close. He knew her body was still sore and healing, so his touch was gentle and careful.

"Come here. What's wrong, baby?" He whispered in the darkness.

She tried to speak but sobbed instead. She rolled over and into him, into his arms, and into his whole being. There with him, she was home. No matter where they were in this world, whether at a rooftop bar in the rain, in their house, or out on the lake, he was her home.

"Shhh, I got you." He touched his lips to her forehead just as he had done when she birthed his son. Suddenly she felt something good. But for only a moment.

"Everything feels foreign. Even you sometimes. I hate it. I don't even feel like this is my body."

Her breathing slowly calmed as he stroked her hair and held her close. So close that she could feel his heart beating.

"It's like I felt so much joy just yesterday, and when I woke up this morning, the joy was gone. I want to be alone, but then I need to be with you and Benjamin, but then I'm still lonely. Nothing makes sense."

Her voice even sounded foreign as she spoke. But saying the words out loud felt like she was removing heaviness from her soul.

"You became a mother, Ivy, to our son. You carried him inside of you for nine months. Everything you did during that time was for him. And for me. For us. And then you brought him into this world. Your body inside out is tired. And you're still doing everything for him and me. This is all new. Everything is different. It feels strange now, but give yourself a little time—a little time to rest and heal. I'm right here. Whatever you need from me, I am here. I always will be."

Her muscles relaxed, her heart rhythm slowed to match his, and she felt light as a feather. She let herself fall asleep because she knew that Liam was there to catch her.

Chapter Five

NOW

As soon as the school bell sounded, it was like magic; in an instant, the playground fell silent as the children rushed inside. Ivy stayed behind; she watched the abandoned swings slow and eventually pause completely. She noticed one single basketball rolling across the blacktop court. The sound from her heels differed greatly from the sound of her gym shoes two decades ago. Not much has changed, yet everything has changed. She used to walk these halls as a student, and now this playground is where she works. She kneeled, picked up the worn ball, walked over to the free throw line, just as she had in the fifth grade many moons ago, and bounced the ball once, then twice. After positioning her hands on the rough leather, she bent her knees, straightened her back, tightened her stomach muscles, took a deep breath, focused on the faded square on the backboard then shot the ball. Swish. The sound of the ball going through the net was the same, but everything else was different. Her body felt different. The air leaving her lungs felt different. It felt silly now to leave her arm in the air with her wrist arched after releasing the basketball.

She couldn't remember the last time she even played a game of *Horse*. Wait, yes, she could. It was in the driveway with Liam. Ivy closed her eyes, took a deep breath in, then slowly out and let the memory have her.

"Two seconds left in the game, she goes left, no, she goes right. Liam does his best to play defense, but it's not enough, ladies and gentlemen!" Ivy sneaks past her husband and makes the layup! "The crowd goes wild! Ivy wins the game!" Before she can say anything else, Liam grabs her from behind. "Ewe! Liam, you're so sweaty! Stop!" Ivy wiggles and tries to get away, but he's stronger. He turns her around, tickling her sides, and continues rubbing his wet bare skin to hers as she laughs.

"Liam!" She tries to say more than his name, but she can't. She's laughing too hard.

"Okay, okay, I'll stop. Kiss me." He lowers her to the ground; her gym shoes stand firm on the driveway. Their chests are rising and falling; they're panting, trying to slow their hearts. Ivy does as she's told, and she kisses him. She pulls him close, sweat and all. The moon is high, the breeze is welcome, all they can hear are the crickets, and all they feel is a thirst to taste one another.

Stop. Ivy opens her eyes. *Don't do this.* She demands her mind to stop recalling memories of Liam. Suddenly she's no longer in her husband's arms in their driveway one late summer night as their son slept in his bedroom taken over by dinosaurs. She's alone, using her planning period on her first day of work to think of Liam. "You're pathetic, Ivy." She harshly whispered to herself. She picked up the ball one last time, shot it, missed it, and then tried her best not to cry as she walked back to her new classroom.

Thankfully, the day passed quickly; it's spring, so summer break is coming soon. But that also means the students are ready to escape the classroom and soak up some sunshine, to sleep until after the sun rises, and to stay up a little later after it goes down. Ivy gets it. She was a student once. Not so long ago, actually.

Just after her third-grade class is dismissed to go home, Ivy walks them to the cafeteria, where they go to their designated bus lines and wait their turn to go out the doors and load the buses. Then she walks back to her classroom on the second floor. It's quiet again. Her heels are noisy again. She's lonely again.

"Ivy!" Ivy hears her name bolted out by another teacher but jumps as if it were Brandy Fowler, Ivy's seventh-grade bully. She grabs her chest, her eyes are wide, and she would like to smack the tall, skinny woman laughing in front of her.

"I'm so sorry, Ivy! I didn't mean to scare you. I heard you coming down the hall with those clodhoppers and just wanted to see how your first day went?"

Immediately annoyed, Ivy collected her composure, calmed her breathing, and faked a smile. "Like riding a bike, thank you for asking, Ms. Fowler." She started toward her classroom, still bearing Mrs. Justice's name on the large wooden door. You see, Ivy has extreme feelings of dislike for Ms. Fowler. She has for a long time.

"Please, call me Brandy. I mean, we live on the same street, silly. Anyway, I wanted to see if you'd like to sign up for something on Field Day?"

"Field Day?" Ivy didn't slow down or even pause, yet Ms. Fowler followed.

"On the last day of school, the students bring money to play different games, buy snacks and just hang outside all day."

"I'm sorry, Ms. Howler..." Oh no, she froze. She said, "*Howler*," not "*Fowler*." Oh goodness. Ivy felt her cheeks grow red as she watched Brandy's cheeks grow redder. "I'm sorry, I mean Ms. Fowler."

"Brandy! You can call me Brandy." The beautiful woman with perfect everything interrupted her. It was no secret that Brandy would sniff out Liam from the crowd at every neighborhood gathering and then flirt with him as if Ivy wasn't right there, holding on to his arm, wearing his ring, or holding their child. Everyone noticed, and Ivy hated it. Liam and Ivy had a little too much to drink one year at a New Year's Eve Party, and Ivy mentioned that, in her opinion, their neighbor resembled a canine. She then announced to their close friend group that Ms. Howler was approaching and made a barking sound. They all found this hilarious, including Liam. And the name stuck. Their friend group referred to her as this ever since. Once she got wind of this, Brandy stopped making passes and coming on to Liam. Ivy was proud of herself for nipping that one in the bud.

But now, their classrooms are beside one another. They are neighbors both at home and work. Yay.

"I have a substitute teacher covering for me that day, Brandy. Maybe next time." Ivy quickly entered her classroom and closed the door, sighing in relief to be rid of her annoying nemesis.

Just as she reached her desk, her phone vibrated. There's always an initial thought, a wonder, a hope that maybe it's Liam. Not, of course, what she used to receive, for example, "Hi baby, I can't wait to get home tonight. I miss you," Or, "I can't stop thinking about you. I love you." But maybe, just a "Hey, how was your day?" or "Just wondering if you or the kids need anything? You, okay?" Those are the new texts Ivy usually receives from time to time when she needs them most.

She's disappointed when she sees that the message is not from her ex-husband but the new man in her life. Joseph is just a friend. As cliché as that sounds, it's true. Everyone, Liam included, thinks it's not true, but it is. His lips have never touched hers. They have spent many hours sharing things about their lives, hopes, and regrets, but they've never shared one another's bodies.

"Just wanted to see how your first day of school went. Didn't get sent to the principal's office already, did you?"

Ivy felt a smile form, not a big one, just a hint of one. "Day was good. I didn't have to see Principal Baird, but Josie K. did."

"And why did you get poor little Josie K. in trouble?"

"Poor little Josie K. got herself in trouble for being disruptive and rude." "Hopefully, she learned her lesson."

"Doubt it." She laughed when she read his message.

Her fingers tapped at the keyboard. Ivy read the sentence she had just typed, then quickly deleted the message. But then she thought of going home to her quiet house. This evening her kids will be picked up from daycare by their dad. She wondered what Liam would make them for dinner. She didn't worry, though. Liam is an exceptional father; he makes the best food and is loyal to their agreement on the kid's schedules and things like snacks, bath time, and bedtime. There is so much Ivy could go home and do. She needs to put away laundry, finish that series on television she began watching two weeks ago, or visit Tia. No, Tia is having a going away celebration dinner and drinks with her friends from work.

She didn't hesitate this time. She typed the message and hit send. She didn't even pause to check for errors or grammatical mistakes.

"Yes." He replied just as quickly.

Ugh. Of course, he said, "Yes." What has she done? Apparently, Joseph is coming to her house for dinner. Great. Maybe she will make up an excuse to cancel? Perhaps she won't answer the door, and then when she sees him next time, she will tell him she fell asleep. No. She promises herself that she won't cancel. She has a date.

Chapter Six

NOW

Liam breathes her in as the friction between her skin and his becomes more intense. Pleasure floods their bodies, drowning all thoughts of anything or anyone away. But he knows it's only temporary. Liam is already somewhere else as soon as he lets go of her, maybe even sooner. She says the right things, but the words are sour. Scarlett's moves are forgettable. She leaves no impression on his body, heart, or soul. He's never portrayed otherwise. She knows. Yet she stays, she tries, and she never complains. She's waiting, and he knows it. She will be waiting forever, he thinks.

The woman in his arms cries out, but he holds it in. He squeezes his eyes shut and forces the pain down deep inside. Every time, his soul goes a little darker.

He feels the darkness until the hot water in the shower washes her away. Even then, some of that darkness remains.

He wonders if he will ever not feel this way with a woman who isn't his ex-wife. Liam squats down in the shower, and the soap suds clear away from his skin. He covers his face with his hands, breathes deeply, and holds it. How can you want so badly to keep something yet also want it to go away at the same time? It took five seconds to love her, but it's taking a hell of a lot more time than that to unlove her. What if it takes all the time he has left? What then?

The bathroom door opens, and steam escapes the small bathroom into Scarlett's small bedroom.

"Hey babe, I've got to get back to work; lock up when you leave?" Scarlett rushes around the bathroom, gathering her makeup that she will throw on in the car using her rear-view mirror. She's the kind of woman that doesn't require makeup; she's beautiful.

"Yep, drive safe." He stands and runs his hands through his dark hair.

He hears her pause, then comes to him. She doesn't pull back the cheap vinyl liner. He feels awful for not having more to say. He knows what she needs to hear. But he can't.

"You, okay?" She's concerned; she cares—more than she should.

"I'm all good, just hurrying so that I can get the kids from daycare in time. I don't want to be late."

It's quiet, and he knows she's going to ask. And she knows the answer will be "no," like always.

"Any dinner plans?" He can hear her holding her breath as she waits for his answer.

He grows frustrated. "Not yet, Scar."

Silence consumes the tiny space.

"Of course. Call me after you put them to bed?"

"I will." His voice is low.

"Bye, Liam." She whispers.

And then she's gone. And he's all alone.

Chapter Seven

THEN

Ivy ran her fingers over the tiny pale pink piece of clothing. It was soft, and the material already smelled like a baby somehow. The same day that she and Liam watched those two lines appear on the test, she bought this little sleeper. She couldn't resist. That same day, she also prayed. And screamed. And cried. Liam didn't show it, but Ivy could feel it. She could feel his insides tangling into a knot. It showed on his face. He smiled, too, though, as did she. Benjamin was their world. They adored every little bit of him. So, they wanted this baby. She breathed in the sleeper one more time and remembered when she said the words the day put up the Christmas tree. Liam turned on Rudolph, and Ivy made hot chocolate. Later that night, Liam carried the exhausted two-and-a-half-year-old to his bed upstairs and tucked him in as tight as a bug in a rug. He came back and sat beside her on the couch. The room was dark, except for the tree lights and the shadows from the fire that danced on the walls across the room.

He kissed her first. Tenderly. They made love slowly, passionately. And just as it was time for Liam to pull away, she asked him not to. "Liam. Don't stop." She whispered, but he heard her loud and clear. He knew by the look in her eyes what she was saying.

"Are you sure?" he asked, breathing hard, trying to be quiet, trying to refrain.

"Yes, I'm sure," she answered.

He kissed her softly, and he didn't stop.

And now, they will find out if their second child is a boy or a girl. Ivy will be ecstatic either way, but as she folds and puts away the little girl's sleeper back into the bottom drawer in their bedroom, she admits that it would be nice to have a daughter. But another little boy will be just as sweet.

Her watch chimed; it was nearly 4 pm. She's supposed to meet Liam in fifteen minutes and must leave now.

When Ivy arrived at the park next to the river, she was relieved to see no one else was there. No one, except Liam. There he was, sitting on their bench by the water. He stood when he saw her pull up, and she nearly sprinted to him.

"Hey, you." His voice never failed to turn all the iciness inside of her back to warm. No matter the day, he fixed her. But today was bittersweet. Every second since her husband kissed her tummy after they learned she was pregnant, they were terrified but didn't say so.

Ivy couldn't help but smile when Liam pulled her close. When he let go of her, he handed her a bouquet of pale pink roses mixed with baby's breath. "Liam. I love them." She brought the soft petals to her nose and breathed them in. "Thank you, baby."

"I'm the one who is thanking you, Ivy. You're having our second child. And I know that this wasn't a decision you made lightly."

"What if it happens again?" Tears were there in one blink. As if they had been on reserve for the past two months, just waiting to be released.

"If it does, we will get through it together."

"I'm scared." She whispered as the river flowed beside them. The air was chilly, but neither had noticed.

"I'll take care of you, just like last time. We will be prepared. I promise."

She kissed him. How is it possible that she gets to be this man's wife?

Liam pulled the envelope from the inside pocket of his sports coat.

Their eyes met. Liam could see hers fill with worry, "It's okay, baby, I've got you. I've got us."

He handed the envelope to her. She carefully ripped the paper across the top and then looked back at her husband.

"It's okay." He whispered, then smiled and gave her a wink.

Her fingers didn't fumble, even though her body trembled. She didn't know if it was because of the winter air or the fear. Either way, her hands were shaking. She removed the folded paper and offered it to Liam.

"You do the honors, Mrs. Cameron." He insisted, and she felt like she was at the top of a rollercoaster, about to go over the hill and then upside down through the loop. But she didn't hesitate; she unfolded the white paper and read its only word.

"Girl." She announced faintly with happy tears.

"Girl? We're having a girl?" Liam's whole face lit up.

"Yes, it's a girl."

Liam rose to his feet and brought Ivy with him. His lean, muscular body raised her high into the air as she laughed. Just like that, he stole it all away; the harrowing memories and the worry. Gone. Just like that. Maybe not gone, but he sent them away to hide. If they were going to come out into the light, Liam and Ivy would be ready. Liam said so.

He lowered her and pulled her in. They swayed back and forth. The river played a lovely melody for them to move to as the sun set for the evening behind them. The way they felt that night on the rooftop, in one another's arms, like this, was exceptional. They both knew it. And they both knew they would never forget it, just like they would never forget this moment; not the surprise of having a daughter, not the sunset, not the song sung by the river, nor the promises, and especially not the pale pink roses.

Chapter Eight

NOW

"I don't know which are your favorites. I hope you like them." Joseph didn't stutter, but she could tell that he was both nervous and excited to see her.

Ivy was surprised by how attractive Joseph looked on her front doorstep tonight. She wasn't surprised that she hated his flowers. Only one man had ever given her flowers; receiving them from anyone else feels wrong. She smiled anyway as she accepted them. "Hi Joseph, please come in. And thank you for these." The last part struggled to come out.

Once inside, Ivy nervously hurried to the kitchen to find a vase for the flowers. She opened the lower cupboard beneath the coffee pot. Two vases. Both had been given to her by her ex-husband. She went to the pantry, where three beautiful vases were sitting on the top shelf, all from Liam.

Ivy closed her eyes and took a deep breath. She would find a large glass to suffice, throw out all the vases tomorrow and buy a new one.

"Here, let me help you with that." Joseph stepped into the pantry with little effort and reached up high to retrieve the middle vase.

"Here you go." The pantry light was off, and Joseph stood close to her. She could feel the heat radiating from his body. She needed out. But she hesitated. Her hand grazed his as she took the vase that Liam brought her flowers in on their last anniversary together. Joseph's lips were plump and near. He must have licked them recently because the bottom one was still wet.

She snapped back to reality. "Not this one." She looked down at the heavy glass in her hands. It was rigid and had precise carvings. It was beautiful. It was also given to her by her husband after he screwed another woman. "Actually, on second thought, this one is perfect." She smiled and left the pantry.

As she carefully placed the array of different colored roses into the vase, she couldn't help but notice that there were two red roses, three white roses, and one pink rose. She didn't add the pale pink rose to the vase. Instead, she crumpled it up with the mess and tossed it into the trash back in the pantry. "There, perfect." Joseph didn't seem to notice.

Her heart was racing. Joseph had helped move things to storage, hung out on the back patio, and they grilled steaks. He had even helped with the kids on occasion. But they had been friends. They had always been in the same friend group, but this was more. Him being here. Like this. He was putting flowers in her husband's vase. This was bigger. She could tell by the way her body reacted to him now.

"Whatever you're cooking smells great." Ivy came back to life. She was like a high school girl standing beside her crush at a pep rally.

"Thank you! I hope you like delicate dishes complimented by fine wine?"

He looked impressed and still so handsome. "Just kidding. It's baked spaghetti and garlic bread. I'm a horrible cook. In fact, I try not to."

Joseph laughed, and Ivy noticed his chiseled chin, dark eyes, and straight teeth.

"I must be pretty special if you're cooking this for me then." He flirted.

She melted, "You are special, Joseph."

Ivy tucked a loose strand of dark hair behind her ear. She hates when her hair is down. Usually, on any other day, it would be in a messy bun. Kimber liked pulling at it, and Ivy didn't like how it itched at the back of her neck or shoulders, but Liam always liked her long hair. He told her so all the time. "Our friend group has dwindled these past few months, but you're still here. You've listened, encouraged, and stuck around when it got awkward for everyone else. You didn't scurry away. I appreciate that. I appreciate you."

"You don't have to thank me. We've been friends a long time, Ivy, but you've always been Liam's wife. I'd be lying if I said I never noticed how you ensured everyone had their favorite songs on the playlist, whether we were just hanging out in the backyard or on the lake. I noticed when you smiled and when you didn't. It's a shame when you don't." His face was close to hers now. She could smell his aftershave. "But you belonged to Liam, and he was the luckiest man in the room. But I still noticed you." His hand touched her cheek; nothing was calculated. Nothing was predictable. She didn't expect to want so badly for him to kiss her. And when he did, she immediately thought of Liam. She was still Liam's. Joseph just didn't know it.

The doorbell rang, then the front door opened. Before Ivy could even distinguish just how close her body was to Joseph, how deep their kiss was, or where her hands were on the man standing in her kitchen… Liam was there with them, holding their baby girl in his arms.

Ivy jumped back as if Joseph was on fire. She didn't know why she jumped. She liked Joseph. And Liam had given her away a long time ago.

Ivy first noticed the redness that collected in Liam's gut and then traveled up his neck and onto his face. His jaw was tight. For a second, it appeared he had forgotten that he was holding little Kimber, wrapped in her white blankie covered in pink ballet slippers. His eyes stared fiercely at the man who used to be both Ivy and Liam's friend, standing in his house, kissing his ex-wife.

"What's wrong with Kimber?" Panic choked Ivy as she rushed to her daughter.

Liam's focus on Joseph broke, and he looked down at the little body in his arms. "She's running a fever," Liam cleared his throat and refused to look at Ivy as she reached for their child, "I gave her Tylenol and a lukewarm bath, but she's still warm."

The oven timer went off just as Ivy felt her one-and-a-half-year-old's hot skin. Ivy noticed Liam watching Joseph maneuver around the kitchen, and he was furious again. He had no right to be; they both knew it.

"Let's take her upstairs and give her some ibuprofen. Where's Ben?" Ivy couldn't get Liam to look at her.

"He's asleep in the truck."

Joseph had set the glass dish full of spaghetti, sauce, and melted cheese onto the stove and turned off the oven. He removed the buffalo-checkered oven mitts and started toward the front door. "I'll go get him."

"I don't think so." Liam's voice sounded foreign to Ivy. He was the angriest she had ever seen him as he left the house to go back to get their son and bring him inside.

"Here, let me help you get her upstairs." Joseph grabbed the diaper bag, blanket, and sippy cup, then followed Ivy up to the master bedroom, where she laid Kimber on the bed. She was just beginning to stir when Liam entered the room. Joseph handed Ivy the warm washcloth she had asked him to get for her.

"I think we have it from here. You can go." Liam didn't ask; he demanded. Unfairly.

Ivy was thankful that Ben was asleep in Liam's arms.

"I don't think you get to say when he has to leave, Liam." Ivy was insulted. Joseph had been there when Liam wasn't. He was her friend, and he was her guest. She got to say when he left.

"It's okay, Ivy," Joseph whispered. "I'll call and check on you in a bit, see if you need anything. He reached over and kissed the top of her head.

The room felt chaotic as Liam stepped aside to allow Joseph to pass by and leave.

Liam waited until they heard the front door close, and then he carried Ben to his bed.

Ben wasn't heavy, but still, Liam's arms shook. He knew it wasn't from carrying his child but from the anger swirling through his veins. He messed up and was immediately regretting how he acted. He couldn't explain it, though. And he was barely able to control it. But he did his best.

He pulled back the dinosaur comforter and tucked his nearly four-year-old son in bed. He stopped and looked around the room. He remembered the day he painted this room a gray-blue color. Ivy had told him everything to get and how she wanted the room to look. He returned from the paint store and painted away; she was so surprised when she got home and saw he had finished it. The next afternoon they hung the pictures and put the baby bed together. It feels like yesterday, yet another life ago. He kissed his son and whispered good night.

When Liam made it back to his former bedroom, which he once shared with his wife, Ivy was lying on the bed next to Kimber.

"She took the medicine and drank a little of her water. I can already tell that she's cooling down. I'll call the doctor's office in the morning and have her checked for an ear infection."

Liam was quiet. His voice had run away. He was embarrassed. He was also thankful Ivy was such a good mother to their kids. But he was mostly regretful.

"I'll call you tom..."

"I could stay." Liam wanted to beg her. He didn't want to leave. He wanted to make sure Kimber was okay. He wanted to be here… with his family."

"You need to go, Liam."

He could tell Ivy was trying not to cry. He had upset her. Again.

"I'm sorry, Ivy. I'm sorry for how I acted and treated Joseph. It wasn't fair."

She didn't reply. She swiped away a tear and readjusted the washcloth on Kimber's warm forehead.

"I miss you, Ivy. Everyday." He nearly choked as he said what he said. He wanted her so badly to say something. Anything. Well, anything besides what she said.

"Just go, please." She was crying now.

He wanted to go to her. He wanted to hold her. But he did what she asked, and he left.

Chapter Nine

Dispatcher:	"911, what's your emergency?"
Caller:	(quiet, distant moaning)
Dispatcher:	"Are you in trouble?"
Caller:	(whimpering)
Dispatcher:	"Where are you? What's the address?"
Caller:	"Help me."
Dispatcher to Authorities:	"Appears to be female. She is crying. She whispered that she needs help. Please hold for location and request paramedics.
Dispatcher:	"Ma'am, are you hurt?"
Caller:	"They're gone."
Dispatcher:	"Who is gone?"
Caller:	(Sobbing) "My kids."

Dispatcher to Authorities:	"Female states that her kids are gone."
Dispatcher:	"Ma'am, where are you? Where did your kids go?"
Caller:	"Riverside Park."
Dispatcher to Authorities:	"Riverside Park. Repeat. Riverside Park"
Dispatcher:	"How old are the children?"
Caller:	(Silence)
Dispatcher:	"Are you still there?"
Caller:	(Silence)
Dispatcher to Authorities:	"Line intact, caller not responding.
Dispatcher:	"Ma'am, we have help coming to you.
Caller:	(Whispering)
Dispatcher:	"What's your name?"
Caller:	(Incoherent Whispering) "Oliver."
Dispatcher:	"Did you say, Oliver? Is your last name Oliver?"
Caller:	(Whispering-low voice) "River…check the river."
Dispatcher:	(Pause) (Clearing her voice) "Ma'am, your children are in the river?" Did you put your kids in the water?"
Caller:	(LINE DEAD)

Chapter Ten

NOW

A Sunday morning can steal you. It can take you right from your bed if you let it. Before you even open your eyes, it's there, with you, waiting for you to acknowledge what's not about to happen but what will. A Sunday can crawl up your spine, wrap around your neck, and squeeze until you can barely breathe. How can one try to defeat this, one might ask? The answer is simple. You allow the alarm to do its job. The square digital object on the nightstand alarms you to wake up fast, shower, and get to work. It warns you before the day can sneak into the room, fill you up, eat you, and then spit you out. One might curiously ask, "What about Saturdays? Liam doesn't work on Saturdays?" The truth is, Saturdays are busy. Most anyway. Depending on the season, there are different things Liam must do. For example, he helps his friend, Drew, coach basketball at the local high school in the winter. In the spring, he has golfing tournaments. He mows his lawn in the summer and hikes or fishes in the fall. But when that sun goes down on Saturday night, it feels like a completely different one that rises on Sunday. The air is thicker, making it harder to breathe. The clock ticks to a different rhythm. It's slower, nearly stopping sometimes.

It wasn't always like this for Liam. He learned fast. He's smarter now. He knows better. He's proactive. And this Sunday isn't any different.

The glowing neon red numbers turn to 7 am. The alarm warns that time is running out and it's coming. Sunday is coming. Liam breathes in deeply and then breathes out slowly after silencing his lifesaver. He doesn't take the time to look around the room, rub his eyes, or stretch. He's up. He makes a beeline to the shower, which isn't far in his small rental home. It's three bedrooms, but barely. The water gets hot quickly though, and so lemons and all that. Liam invites the steam to engulf him. And it does. He's hurting all over, inside and out. Not necessarily his muscles, his joints, nor his bones; it's his whole being. Every single vessel. Every time he dips his head forward beneath the stream of water, he closes his eyes. And every time, the darkness brings Ivy. Ivy is in their kitchen with him. He must again close his eyes when he moves the hot, soapy washcloth over his face. And there is Ivy, again, as if the memory was there just waiting for him. She's holding their sick little girl in her arms, and she knows all the things, all the things to do to make her better. And he's on the outside. She won't let him in. And he deserves it.

Oh no, Sunday is lurking. "Stop, Liam, stop," Liam whispers. He knows that thoughts of his ex-wife create portals for Sunday to take him at any time or place.

In a few minutes, Liam has brushed his teeth, dressed, and is heading out his wooden front door. The air pods in his ears are blaring, and this is when he really wakes up. This is when Liam comes alive, and he knows that he's surviving a Sunday as long as there are no portals. He vows in this moment... "No portals." His heart pumps faster, and his lungs contract and expand harder as his expensive black running shoes pound the concrete. He's free. He knows it's probably just temporary, though. There's a portal that's coming. One he can never control, no matter how hard he tries.

The North Carolina air is crisp, and the sky is clear this beautiful morning. Five miles will be a breeze. He follows the windy, two-lane road for a mile. He makes a right onto the trail that runs by the river for half a mile, then exits the forest at Riverside Park and does three laps around the narrow walking path over the grounds, which equals another mile. He then heads onto another road back home. Five miles total. The most difficult part of Liam's run occurs during the end stretch home after he leaves the park. It's not because the road has hills that feel like small mountains. It's not because the sun is beating down and he's drenched in sweat. It's because of the place. Every time Liam sees it coming up ahead of him, his feet slow, and his body calms. By the time he reaches the small and quaint little white building with stained glass windows and a gravel parking lot, he's walking. And every time, the steeple greets him like an old friend. It sounds like an angel is touching the keys of a piano, sending the notes straight to God himself. And she is. She is an angel. He can't see her but can if he closes his eyes. She's sitting on the stool, wearing a long champagne-colored skirt that sways when she walks. Strands of shiny, black hair that Liam used to run his fingers through as she rested her head on his chest while they watched tv, nearly touching the small of her back. His kids sit in the front row near their mama at the piano. Being loved and cared for by their old friends they sit with every Sunday morning because Liam is out here. Now sitting Indian style next to the tall old oak tree, listening; hurting; regretting; remembering with his eyes closed. There's that portal. And just like that, he's swallowed up and taken by another Sunday.

Chapter Eleven

THEN

"One. Two. Three. Four. Five. Six. Seven."

Kimber's little smiling face excitedly looked at her mother as they heard the counting getting closer to ten. Ivy's heart skipped a beat at the cuteness. She squeezed the little girl hiding with her in the tiny wooden playhouse.

"Eight. Nine. Ten! Ready or not, here we come!"

Both Ivy and Kimber anticipated footsteps coming closer outside. They listened and tried not to breathe too loudly. Strangely Ivy suddenly needed to pee, but she would have to wait.

"We found you! I did it, Daddy; I found Mama and Kimby!" Benjamin jumped up and down as Liam patted his head, smiling.

"Good job, buddy!"

"Awe, you found us! Darn, it." Ivy reached out and tickled her son's little tummy.

"Again! Again!" Benjamin's bare feet danced around in the grass and dirt.

"Okay, this time, you have to hide." Ivy crawled out with her giggly one-year-old still in her arms.

"Hide, and I'll count to ten!"

"Liam and their son, with olive skin and dark brown wavy hair that covered his ears, ran away as Ivy closed her eyes and began to count slowly.

"One. Two. Three. Four. Five." Ivy paused to listen. Usually, she could hear Ben's little nervous giggle and shuffle in his hiding spot. But it was silent. All she could hear were the birds chirping in the tree beside her, the humming of a lawnmower in the distance, and the spilling of water from their pool filter. She peeked; it was against the rules, but she was curious and needed to check on Kimber. The tiny tot was still sitting on the picnic blanket, drinking from her sippy cup.

Ivy closed her eyes and continued… "Six. Seven. Eight. Nine. Ten! Ready or not, here…" A startling roar came from behind her, and before she could even open her eyes to see or her mouth to cry out, she was in the air. Liam held on tight as he swung his wife around and around without her feet touching the ground. She laughed as he tickled her sides, then lowered her to the ground. She felt the soft, itchy grass on the back of her neck and bare legs.

"Liam, stop!" The words barely escaped her as his fingers tickled her sides.

"We tricked you, Mama! We tricked you!" Benjamin danced and ran around them, holding tight to his metal die-cast silver airplane in his right hand. It's his favorite toy. Ever. Ivy must snatch it while he sleeps to wash away the germs. Then she puts it back safely before he wakes.

"You sure did; that was not nice. You scared me!" Her chest quickly rose and fell as she tried to catch her breath.

Ben ran to the slide near his sister, still playing on the soft, rope-knitted cream-colored blanket.

"I got you good." Liam was equally as out of breath.

Ivy looked over at him as he lay beside her in the grass. She noticed the big smile he was wearing and his hand still holding onto hers.

She tried to remember everything she had read. She recited it all quickly, silently. "Number One, don't put her in the room. She's not physically there with the two of you; don't invite her to be present in your hearts or minds. Don't say her name." Before she could move on to the number two, Liam's kind, blue eyes met her own. He instantly knew. And just like that, there are three of them lying there. Liam knows, and his smile fades. There's an unspoken gentleness between them. A healing wound has been picked at. And now there's a little pain, a slight fear of never getting better, and some frustration. Liam pulls her close, and she lets him. She allows him to hold her in his arms. He kisses the skin over her temple and rests his head on the ground beneath them. He's sorry, and she knows it.

Chapter Twelve

NOW

"I think it's hilarious that we only have two members in our infamous book club. You and me." Tia laughed as she added the romance novel to her pale peach-colored backpack.

"You know that I am anti-social now. Besides, who needs more friends when we are as cool as we are?" Ivy smelled the candle sitting on the bar, and the aroma of Praline Waffles filled her senses.

"Ready!" Tia announced, zipping up her bag and slinging it over her shoulder.

"Shall we go to Coffee, Scones, and Books...Oh, My! or should we try that sweet little café on the corner? Both places have outdoor seating. It's your turn to pick, and can I just say I am very thankful it will be my turn to pick the book soon because this one is the worst."

"What?! You usually love my book choices?!" Ivy returned the candle to the place on the counter where she got it from.

"I just don't like it. I don't know why exactly."

Ivy noticed as her friend fidgeted with one of the many packed boxes scattered throughout the living room. "It's difficult for me to read novels like this one sometimes as well. It brews up a lot of things from the past, then it smells like burnt coffee and tastes like shit. We don't have to finish it if you don't want?"

"I'd like that very much. Thank you." Tia looked relieved.

"In fact, let's not read at all. Let's go on an adventure!" Ivy clapped and jumped up and down like a high school girl.

"Oh no, you have that crazy look in your eyes." Tia let her bag hit the floor with a thud.

Taken aback, Ivy's mouth grew wide, "What crazy look?!"

"That exact one you are wearing right now."

"I can't be too long; Kimber has an ear infection. The sitter came over after church and said she could stay most of the day, but I hate not being with Kimber when she doesn't feel well." Ivy slipped into her sandals with light brown leather straps.

"I thought they were with their dad this weekend. Tia tied the laces to her white gym shoes with black stripes.

"Oh, did I forget to tell you about the eventful night I experienced with both Joseph and Liam?!"

"You certainly did forget to tell me. I'd love to hear all about it."

"I'll give you all the details in the car on the way. Let's go!"

Once in Ivy's black Tahoe, they did stop by the Coffee, Scones, and Books…Oh My! and both chose iced lattes.

"I thought you said you were moving on once the divorce was final? That other than co-parenting, you were done with Liam?"

"I am done; it's just that when I'm with Joseph, I only compare him to Liam. Nothing tastes as sweet; nothing feels as natural, and nothing makes me want to run out the door faster and run back to my husband."

"Ex-husband." Tia stared out of her passenger window as she sipped on her latte.

"You're right. Ex-husband."

"I don't mean to be so cold; it's just that I have seen this before. I don't want you to lose an opportunity with a great man just because you're holding on to false hope with a relationship that has been over for a long time."

"You're right. And trust me, I don't want to feel this way. It was a big step having Joseph over to the house." Ivy felt herself becoming defensive. "I don't think anyone understands this. You've never been married, Tia, let alone divorced, with two children. It's the hardest thing in the world. You lose, every day, no matter what. When Kimber does something for the first time, and I look over to share that moment with Liam, he's not there. I'm alone. When Ben cries for his dad because he misses him, I hold him and try my best not to cry right along with him because I miss him too. I have to look strong. I can't cry until I'm alone. Liam was special. We were special. And I know you didn't get to see us in that way, but it was something from a fairytale. Until it wasn't." Even now, while the kids are back home and Ivy is turning off the main highway onto a side road in the middle of nowhere, she won't let herself cry. Not in front of Tia.

"You're going to find another prince, Ivy. One that won't hurt you." Tia kept her voice low.

"It won't be the same. I hate her. More than I've ever hated any one person or thing. I hate her." Ivy surrendered and let the tear slide down her cheek. She couldn't help it.

Tia touched Ivy's right arm. It didn't fix anything, but it offered a little comfort. It did throw all the angst out the window. She had nothing to forgive Tia for, she was only trying to help, but Ivy forgave her anyway.

The side road then narrowed after a sharp curve. They hadn't passed a house, barn, or even an old grown-up homeplace for miles now. The Tahoe turned right onto a one-lane gravel road full of potholes and grass that grew in the middle on the part of the road that tires never touch.

"Where in the world are we going?!" Tia held on tight to her splashing iced drink and her door.

"We are going to my cabin. I never come out here, especially since the kids came along, except to dust a little and put out poison for the mice and other critters that trespass inside."

"Trespass? Like there are critters inside of the place we are going?"

"It's good that you are leaving the North Carolina country and returning to the city. This is awesome! You'll see."

Tia rolled her eyes and smiled. "You're not wrong."

It only took a few more moments until the road ended. A small wooden cabin peeked out from behind the trees and overgrowth. "This looks like something out of a scary movie, Ivy."

"This is my parents' little place. We came here all the time when I was a kid."

Ivy and Tia unbuckled their seat belts and got out of the SUV. Tia's eyes were wide with wonder. Ivy's heart felt full. "I think I'm going to have someone come and clean up all the overgrowth so the kids can play. I always wished I had a sister or a friend to be here with me to play. But it was always just me."

"That sounds very lonely."

"It was."

"Well, look at you now." Tia grabbed her friend's hand and gave a little squeeze.

Thankful for her friend being by her side, she smiled. Ivy picked up a sharp rock and walked over to the big tree in what used to be a yard. She carved two lines over one another hard. Then stood back to observe. Beside her name was Liam's. Ivy still remembers the magical day he wrote those letters in the bark. He might as well have written them in her flesh. It felt just as painful today to mark it out. Then Tia held out her hand. "May I?" Tia asked.

Delighted to have her friend's name alongside hers at this special place, she handed her the rock and watched as the woman in black leggings and an off-the-shoulder, oversized white sweatshirt carved the letters T-I-A.

"There. Out with the old, in with the new. Now you have had a friend here. A real friend who cares about you and will never hurt you."

"It's perfect, thank you." Ivy traced the "x" with her fingers as her vision blurred from her tears.

And then a bird swooped down and cried out, scaring both women so much so they screamed. Then they laughed hysterically at one another. Once they caught their breath, Ivy got excited to show Tia everything—every inch of her childhood.

"I want you to come inside, and then we will walk the path to a cave."

"A cave?"

"You will love it; we are on an adventure, remember? It's a beautiful spring day, please?" Ivy didn't mind begging. She wanted her friend to taste just how charming this place was. It's as sweet as sugar.

"Creepy old house, poison ivy-covered path, and then a dark, wet cave full of bats and creatures from hell. When you say adventure, you mean let's test death." Tia was uneasy. Ivy could tell.

"We will take weapons, and it will be fine, I promise." Ivy started toward the cabin. And to Tia's surprise, she followed.

Chapter Thirteen

NOW

I miss you.

Liam read the text over and over as he took a swig of his soothing, cold liquid in the long-neck bottle.

"Want another? The cooler is full?" Shane asked his friend as he flipped burgers on the grill.

"Nah, I'm good, man." Liam pressed the button on the side of his cell phone, and the screen went dark.

"How's everything been at the office in Charlotte?" Liam was curious, as he hadn't set foot back there since the day he was asked to leave. The day his boss, Tanner, confronted him about the "situation" with Scarlett—one of the worst days of Liam's life.

"Man, when I say insane, I mean like mind-blowing mad. Tan has me covering ten or more closings a week. Katy's going to leave me if something doesn't change soon.

I told Tanner that I would start looking for a new gig, no joke." Shane took a long pull from his cold beer and flipped another burger. The sizzling sound hissed.

"I wish I could say the same; I'm getting maybe two at best a week. And it's the high-risk accounts that require ten-hour days. I've had three to fall through in the last month. I'm just struggling. As soon as my contract is up in six months, I will apply at Benson and Benson Finance."

"Do you think Tan will give you a good reference?"

By the way that Shane looked around and lowered his voice, Liam could tell he knew how bad this looked in the professional world. "This" meaning an affair among coworkers.

"I doubt it. And that's okay. It is what it is." Liam scratched at his dark, freshly trimmed beard and readjusted his Wake Forest ball cap.

The sun started sinking, and pink waves splashed across the sky. He heard her laugh before he saw her face. Liam hadn't expected her to be here. And by the look of her doe eyes, she hadn't expected him to be there either. Secrets. It was their foundation.

"Actually, I will take you up on that offer. I need another drink." Liam stood tall in his worn jeans and a dark t-shirt. He needed a haircut; he could feel the dark curls escaping his hat and teasing the tops of his ears. It was driving him crazy.

Shane noticed Scarlett, "Of course, man, help yourself."

Liam did just that; after tossing the bottle into the large trash can, he reached inside the cooler, snatched a drink, and then directed his attention to anyone else.

The music was loud, but not too loud. The firepit was warm, and the laughter was contagious.

It wasn't until she whispered into his ear from behind that he noticed just how late it had gotten. Only stragglers remained. Most had gone home. Some were helping Shane clean up, Justin was strumming his guitar by the fire, and people sang along and swayed, cheering after every song.

"Dance with me." She whispered.

He didn't say it aloud, but he thought of Ivy. *"I don't think they have dancing here,"* She had replied all those years ago on the rooftop bar in the city. His insides were aching for her. It was the first time he heard her voice. Tonight, right now, his insides were tangled, twisted, and on fire. He felt sick.

"Hey. I didn't know you were coming tonight." Liam's bottle was empty. He should go.

"You didn't tell me either. Is that what we are doing now? Keeping secrets?" The tall, curvy woman with shoulder-length strawberry blonde hair, tight-fitting jeans that clings to her hips when she walks, a sleeveless white lace top, and flat sandals that boast her toes painted a pale pink asked quietly. She smelled like something someone would eat for breakfast. Like something sweet.

"I thought the same thing." He replied.

"Come with me." She held out her hand to him. Liam hesitated, but he took it.

He let her lead him beyond the yard and into the trees. The moon was bright now. The sun had gone without saying goodbye. He missed it. The music floated from the guitar into the darkness with them. Scarlett stopped and faced the man she had fallen in love with. "Dance with me. Please?"

She put her hands on the sides of his face, letting his beard tickle her skin. She pulled him near and touched her lips to his. They were already wet. Perfect.

Their bodies began to sway, and after a while, two became one. Liam thought of how differently this woman felt in his arms. It still felt wrong. Because it still is. He should be with someone now that he is divorced, anyone, in fact. Just not Scarlett. Not the woman who he got lost in. It would kill Ivy if she knew. He had hurt her enough, and this would break her. Scarlett can never play with their children or rock them to sleep. It's forbidden. At least it should be. She wants more than this. More than just him. She wants everything, and Scarlett deserves more. More than he has to give her.

He started to speak, and she touched her finger to his lips. "Not tonight. Don't say anything. Just hold me. Be here with me." She whispered, but no one was close enough to hear.

"I know what you're thinking. But we can take it slow. I'll be patient."

Liam took a deep breath, tasting the night air. He missed his wife. He missed the rain. He missed everything.

Chapter Fourteen

THEN

The lake has many versions; it changes all the time. Sometimes in a blink. The sun had been bright this morning, and Liam welcomed the breeze as he drove the boat to their favorite cove. Ivy couldn't help but stare at him from the seat behind him. His shirtless back was tight and kissed by the sun. His ball cap was turned around backward to keep the wind from stealing it, his navy-blue swimming trunks still dry. On his left hand, he wore his wedding ring. Ivy looked down at her bare hand and noticed that the indention from her own circle of gold had faded. There was no longer any evidence of the precious set of rings her husband had so carefully placed on her finger on their wedding day.

The lake was busy. Boats of all kinds came and went as they had lunch, chatted with friends they tied up with for a bit, and then sat silently with their eyes closed, soaking up the sun's rays.

And then, like a snap of a finger, the other boaters had cleared the cove, the sun was retreating, the wind was cool, and the water was no longer still and a kind green. It was now swift and placid, as dark as the clouds looming over them.

"I want a divorce." She said it so calmly, cutting the silence between them like a sharp knife. She watched as Liam, pulling up the anchor with his back to her, paused, not saying a word. His head dropped, and he let go of the anchor, allowing it to fall back onto the bottom of the lake. He turned, sat, and ran his hands through his hair. His face was tight.

She patiently waited for him to speak, to say anything. She needed to hear his voice so she couldn't hear her own heart breaking into a million pieces.

"I thought I could forgive you. I thought I could forget. But I can't. I wish I could."Tears slowly made their way down her cheeks.

"I wish we both could." His voice cracked, and he cleared his throat.

"Is there anything I can do to change your mind? Anything?" Liam rose to his bare feet and kneeled before her, taking her trembling hands into his. She let his kind; blue eyes look into hers for a long time.

"I'm sorry, Ivy. I would take it back if I could. And I will never hurt you again. I swear it." He was desperate for her to believe him.

Flashes of that night flooded Ivy's soul as the rain fell onto her face, reminding her of the raindrops falling that night against the windshield. It was darker and cooler. Two unoccupied car seats were in the back seat. Ivy was dry, but somehow as she drove from one hotel parking lot to the next, looking for her husband's truck, she cried. She had been crying every day since she birthed their six-month-old daughter. Liam had done everything he could, and Ivy knew that. But she had sent him away anyway that day. The fight was the worst they had ever endured. She was broken, and she was working exceptionally hard to break Liam. And now she shattered them into so many pieces that it would be impossible to put them back together again. She could feel it in her veins that night. She was on the outside; somewhere in one of these places, he was inside with her, and she had no idea.

Liam had told her that he was slipping. He was struggling. They needed help. She needed help. He begged her to talk to someone. To do it for the kids, for him… to do it for herself. She was disappearing, and she was suffering. She was sick. She needed help. But she refused. She told him to leave, to take everything and leave. She told him they were over. She told him that she didn't love him anymore. And then he was gone and would travel to places he'd never come back from.

Liam said he was sorry when he told her where he had been and that he wasn't alone. Then everything went dark. Days later, after the light returned, she held him while he cried. He held her hand every day. He tried even harder to take care of her than he did before that night.

Then came strange feelings. Ivy didn't trust him. Mistrust and fear are dangerous for anyone, but Ivy tried her best. She vowed she wouldn't ask if he saw her at work that day. But before the dinner dishes were cleared from the dark wood dining room table, Ivy's mouth was dry, her heart was pounding, and she was asking. She promised herself that she would never look at his phone. She could if she wanted to, he had given her permission to look at it anytime. She didn't even need to ask. When Liam fell asleep, Ivy was wide awake. She searched through every message, contact, app, history, and whatever she could do to help herself breathe more easily. She never found anything, but before she even opened her eyes the following day, the worry was there again, wrapping around her body and soul like a cold, lonely night in winter. And as she pushed the stroller over the blacktop path at Riverside Park, she was distracted by her children's laughter and cries. She only wondered if her husband was with "her." After all, her office was only two offices down from his on the left.

On the way home from the park, the kids would nap, and Ivy found herself in the city. She wondered if Liam was sitting across from her in a meeting inside that building. Did their shoulders touch as they passed in the breakroom? Did she send him non-work-related messages telling him that she missed him? Did he send them to her? She was going crazy. Then she would drive out of the city and straight home, embarrassed, disappointed, and angry. Angry with herself, angry with Liam, and angry at the woman whose skin touched her husband's one dark and stormy night.

And now, here they are, many moons later, on a different stormy night. Both are tired, both are sad, and both are regretful.

"I'm sorry." Ivy's voice cracked as she broke out into a full sob.

"No, no, baby. Don't be sorry. I'm the one at fault here. I messed up, and I can't fix it." He pulled her into his lap and held her tight, burying his face into her neck.

"It's my fault. I destroyed us. I pushed you away, and I told you to leave." She no longer cared if either of them could hear her heart-shattering.

"No, Ivy, you were sick. You had severe postpartum depression, and I should have been a better husband. I should have found a way to help you, not make things worse."

"I love you, Liam." She raised her head, and so did he. They were drenched, much like the night they met. Instead of a rooftop, they sat on the floor of a boat they had bought one sunny summer day. That was a good day, the best day. And this one is the worst.

The lake had changed. The sun had drowned in the dark clouds, and the wind was cold as Liam slowly drove the boat home in the rain. Liam hates this version of the lake. He already missed how the lake looked this morning and always would.

Chapter Fifteen

NOW

The cabin was small but cozy. Hunting vests rested on hooks near the front door. An antler chandelier hung from the ceiling over the old, scratched wooden coffee table on a braided red and green rug.

Ivy led her friend into the kitchen. "This is where my dad used to sit while my mom cooked us bacon and fried eggs. And then when Liam and I came here, I made them for him."

Tia chose to stay silent and let her eyes take in all the originality of such a quaint little place in the middle of nowhere.

"There's two bedrooms down the hall, one bathroom, and a cellar. That's where we kept all the canned food. I'm not sure why they did that. Just the times, I suppose."

Ivy watched Tia as she followed her from room to room. Fascinated and skeptical at the same time.

"Does your family still come here a lot?"

"Not really, only to maintain. When Liam and I were dating, we made love here. A lot. Right there where you are sitting, actually."

Tia jumped to her feet, her eyes big.

"Oh, come on, it's not a big deal." Ivy laughed.

"It's kind of a big deal. Gross." Tia wiped at her bottom as she walked back toward the front door.

"After my dad passed, my mom started working full-time and travels a lot. But she visits us, always brings the best gifts, and makes my favorite meals. Every time I see her, it's like Christmas. She's the best." Ivy's smile faded as she noticed Tia's hurt expression. It didn't take a genius to realize that Tia was probably thinking of her own mother's shortcomings and recent passing.

"Let's get this hike over with." Tia half-joked.

They stayed on the beaten path as they made their way through the briars and weeds. No one said much as they stepped over fallen trees and climbed small boulders. It was obvious that Tia was scared and not having a good time.

"There's nothing to be afraid of. No one is here, and no one will hurt us." Ivy reassured her.

"It's just that I hate heights." Tia looked over the edge. The bottom was far, far away. If she listened hard enough, she could hear her breathing echoing.

The beaten path wasn't so beaten anymore; weeds had taken over most of it. Spider webs clung to their skin as they used their bare hands to move the branches aside. Bees swarmed, and mosquitos were taking full advantage of their unprotected skin. But Ivy didn't mind; this was better than a sad book.

"Liam and I didn't have a lot of time to do things like this before having children, and sometimes I wish we would have. It might have been different if we had waited." Ivy continued leading Tia up the mountainside. The bottom was very far down. They were looking at treetops now. She wouldn't admit it, but she was even a little scared now.

Out of breath and frustrated, Tia eased between a boulder and the mountainside. "Liam hates hiking. I'm not sure you missed out on anything."

"How do you know that Liam hates to hike?" Ivy didn't stop moving forward.

"Well, um, I mean, you've told me before that he didn't like to hike."

The air grew thick, and the songs the birds sang for them filled the awkward silence between the two women. Ivy tried to remember a time when she and Tia might have had such a discussion.

"I think we should go back now. Let's..." Before Tia could finish, she saw Ivy's right foot slip. Her face slammed into a rock that was sticking up from the dirt. It happened so fast. In a blink, Ivy was sliding over the cliff. She was grabbing, reaching for anything that may save her. Tia froze yet was very aware. Ivy was screaming her name. One of her hands was desperately grasping onto a root. The panic and fear in Ivy's eyes will forever remain in Tia's memories.

"Tia! Help me!" Ivy begged; her bloodied face was already bruising. Tears were streaking through the dirt on her cheeks.

Tia shook, and the scream brought her back. She rushed over to Ivy and got a glimpse of what was below. She couldn't breathe. Everything went silent. She could see gravity taking Ivy a little more with every passing second. She would die. Ivy would die and be gone forever if she didn't help her. She slowly reached out her trembling hand. Tia felt weak and nauseous. She sat in the dirt, pulling with all her might. Ivy's broken nails dug into her arm, the skin ripped, and blood appeared.

After one last tug, Ivy was safe. They panted hard while scurrying quickly away from the edge as if something would slither out of hell and drag them over and down into darkness. Both were shaking.

"Ivy, are you okay? Your face is covered in blood!" Tia looked down and saw that Ivy's right foot was swollen and already turning purple. The sun was high in the sky and slicing through the branches, burning their skin and eyes.

"My foot, it hurts so bad."

Ivy was losing consciousness. She was becoming incoherent and disoriented.

"I'm going back to the house; I had service there. I'll call for help and then come right back. I can't get you out by myself."

Tia turned to leave. "Call Liam. Tell Liam we need help. Here's my phone." Ivy couldn't pull her phone from her pocket. Tia helped her and took off back to the car.

Ivy closed her eyes and then touched her face. Tia was right; blood was everywhere. The lights went dark before she could figure out where she was hurt and where the blood was coming from.

It felt like seconds. Like magic. "Ivy, wake up."

Ivy could hear a voice. Relief spread through her like a Sunday morning sitting at the piano. She was saved. Liam had come to take her to a hospital.

"When her foot slipped, she fell, and her face hit a rock. Then she was falling over the edge."

"My foot. Hurts." It was all Ivy could muster.

She felt him pick her up; he was gentle. She rested her head on his chest.

Her head pounded, and her foot throbbed. Her skin burned. She could taste metal; she could taste her blood. He let go of her, gently laying her onto the backseat of his vehicle. "Everything is going to be okay. I'm taking you to the hospital." Ivy opened her eyes as Joseph checked that she was secure one last time.

"Tia, where's Liam? Did you call Liam?" Ivy's lips were swelling and bleeding as well.

"I did call Liam, but he didn't answer," Tia whispered.

Then she squeezed her friend's hand and closed the door. The truck left a cloud of dust from the gravel as it barreled away.

"He didn't answer." Ivy closed her eyes and cried before she let the darkness take her again.

Tia watched Joseph's truck drive down the overgrown, narrow gravel road away from the old cabin, "I know Liam hates to hike because he told me so a long time ago. Long before you, Ivy."

Chapter Sixteen

NOW

"If you care about me, Liam, you will stop being distant and afraid to be seen with me. You're divorced now. Your marriage is over. And I'm sorry about that. I truly am. I swear it. But this back and forth of whatever this is, whatever you want to call it, for the past year, I can't do it anymore. It hurts too bad."

The sound of the pine needles and fresh new spring grass crunched beneath their feet as they swayed. The air had cooled. Liam felt chill bumps spread over Scarlett's skin. He pulled her closer. He held her tighter.

"I wish I could keep you." She whispered. Both figures danced in one another's arms as they realized the guitar had stopped.

She could. Maybe. After all, at one time, it felt like she was saving Liam when he was falling. None of this had ever been her fault. He was already gone when his lips touched hers for the first time. She was just the cherry on top of a crumbling, melting dessert.

Liam kissed her forehead, took her by the hand, and led her out of the woods. When they emerged out of the darkness and into the moonlight, he didn't let go of her, even though she tried to pull her hand away, in fear that everyone sitting around the fire pit would see. Liam glanced back and saw that her eyes were wide. He could be hers. She had been his for a while now. She had carried him; now, he was on his feet, and both hands were free. Free to hold hers.

"Hey guys, have a seat." Shane motioned toward a couple of unoccupied chairs. "Kyle, get in the cooler and grab them a couple of drinks, would you?"

"That's okay. I think we are going to head out. Early day tomorrow. Thanks for having us. Goodnight, everyone." With Scarlett's hand still in his, they left. It was official now. Liam no longer cared what anyone thought about them. He did care about how Scarlett felt, though. He had hurt one person; he didn't want to hurt another.

Once they got back to Liam's rental home, just like before at the party, he held on to Scarlett's hand, and this time he led her to his bed as she followed close behind.

She had been in Liam's home and in his arms many times before, but this time was different. When he closed the door this time, he didn't leave most of him outside in the hall, in the dark. This time he left Ivy on the other side of the closed door.

His touch was gentle, and his kisses were tender. But he had to be honest. He always promised to tell the truth, even when he wasn't asked.

"I have to take this slow. You and me. That finalized paperwork; it doesn't change everything. It probably never will." His voice was low as her worried eyes looked into his. "I'm going to try though, really try. I promise."

She didn't take the time to say anything. She showed her acknowledgment by touching Liam's face, then kissing his warm lips. It was an unspoken understanding. They would take it slow.

Chapter Seventeen

NOW

The last time Ivy woke up in a room like this, she was in much more pain. It was quieter then. No vital monitoring machines were beeping, or IV pumps were dripping. Drip, beep, drip, beep. Over and over. And last time, she was alone. Every muscle ached, and every bone cracked. Reaching with her right hand as the clear IV tubing dangled, she gently touched her face. Her lip was puffy and busted, she had an inch-long cut over her left cheekbone, and her nose was sore. She was having a difficult time tolerating the nasal cannula. A sledgehammer must have drilled her right foot; every time her heartbeat, she could feel it pulsate in her extremity. Overall, according to the paper on the wall, her pain level was one with the face that was sweating, eyebrows creased, and eyes slanted. So, a solid eight. An eight, like she just crawled out of the ring with Mike Tyson using only her arms, kind of eight. But still, she was not in as much pain as the last time.

"Hey there." Joseph sat forward in the chair next to her bed.

"Are the kids okay? Where are they?" Ivy's mouth was so dry that her tongue felt like sandpaper.

"I spoke with the sitter, and she will stay with them tonight. I tried calling Liam about an hour ago, but still no answer. I'll try again in the morning. If he doesn't get the kids, I'll go get them, take them to daycare, and we will figure the rest out later." Joseph carefully moved a dark strand of hair from her face, then offered her a sip from a plastic cup. The cold liquid from the straw was like an answered prayer. Yet, all she could think of was if the kids got their baths, did Ben have anything to drink after six? Did Kimber get her allergy medicine? And lastly, does Liam care about his family at all? What if one of their children was lying in this room, hurt and scared?

"I'm going to go let the nurse know you're awake. I'll be right back." Joseph stood, then moved toward the door.

"Joseph." Ivy's throat felt raw. "Thank you. For coming to my rescue and for staying." She watched his worried, slanted eyes soften.

"Of course. I'm just happy that you're okay." He shot her a wink and then quietly closed the door behind him.

Ivy took a deep breath, then closed her eyes to rest while she waited. But she could still see a sliver of the dimmed overhead light. She reached again with her right hand and dragged the clear IV tubing to feel her throbbing left eye. Just as she suspected, the skin was tender and swollen. "Great,"

Ivy whispered. She felt a swollen inch-sized laceration over her left cheekbone. Both lips were busted and twice as big as usual. Wanting to reposition herself in the stiff hospital bed, she nearly screamed out when she moved her right foot. She was in so much pain she bit at her bottom lip, and more pain shot through her whole body. This time, she let it out. Not a big scream, just a little one. Even now, it remains true that the last time Ivy woke up in a hospital bed, she was hurting more than this.

Joseph and an older woman with gray hair wearing a white coat entered the room. The light from the hallway sent a piercing lightning strike through Ivy's brain. She closed her weary eyes and found a hiding place in the darkness.

"Ivy! Ivy!" She was fading, but she could hear the panic in Joseph's voice. She couldn't speak, but she'd tell him she would be back if she could. She just needed to stay in the darkness for a little while.

This dark place she's in is a familiar one. She's been here before. Except for this time, she's here by choice. This time, she knows how to find her way out and back to the light.

Ivy finds a warm corner. She lowers herself onto the floor. The familiar surface is comforting, like a safe, cozy bed when you're a child on a cold, snowy morning and school has been canceled. Her head rests against the padded wall, and all is well. But she starts to remember the time she was here before and how she got here.

The day was dark. Not as dark as this place, but the storms were coming. Ivy lay in bed for the third day in a row, staring out the window at the rolling, angry clouds.

The leaves on the tree in the front yard were turned upward, begging for a drink.

She could hear Liam pulling into the drive, the motor went silent, and his door opened, then closed. In a few minutes, he would see. See that she is serious.

The front door opens but doesn't close. Ivy imagines that he's noticing all his bags in the foyer. She pulls on her champagne-colored robe and ties the belt loosely, then rushes to the top of the staircase. Ivy finds Liam squatting with his head down and his hands in his hair. He's exhausted, she can tell. She is as well.

"When I said I wanted you to leave, I meant it." Ivy was furious.

"Ivy. I was not calling you crazy this morning. I was just concerned and think we need to get you some help. Why does that make me a horrible husband?!" He stands and kicks the suitcase, and it hits the wall with a thud.

"I don't need help, Liam! I need you to leave!"

Liam places his hands on his hips, his chest rising and falling with anger and sadness. But then he takes a deep breath, and this time, he doesn't yell. This time he can barely even whisper.

"I don't deserve this, Ivy. You did this after you had Ben, and it's worse this time with Kimber. I'm worried about you. I want our life back."

"Well, I don't. I'm sad because I'm unhappy with you. Not from postpartum depression. Why can't you understand that?" Ivy paused and dared her tongue to spit the last words she wanted to say to him out of her mouth. Then she changed her mind, but it was too late to take back the dare. She said them. "I don't love you anymore, Liam."

Liam's head shot up to look at her. She was frozen and couldn't look away. His eyes changed to an icy blue; his face turned pale.

"If I leave, Ivy, I'm not coming back."

Ivy hesitated, holding her breath. She had gone too far. This wasn't like them. They didn't fight; she didn't pack his bags and tell him she didn't love him. But here they are.

"Please, just go." Ivy turned away, returning to the bedroom where she crawled into the bed she had been in for days. She waited. She didn't breathe. She lay as still as she could to hear one of two things. She listened to see if Liam would come upstairs to her or if he would close the door and leave forever. She listened hard, pleading, begging God for Liam to stay. She felt stupid and confused. He was right; he didn't deserve this. She then heard the door quietly close. No footsteps, just the sound of his truck starting and backing down the driveway. There was only the sound of the storm that had finally arrived.

Liam didn't look back; he refused. His heart was pounding as he left the driveway. It had been bad for months, but not like this. This feels absolute. He drove to his office from their little town and into the city. He had plenty of work and a nice couch to sleep on until he figured everything out. It was Friday evening; no one would be in the building until Monday morning.

Liam bypassed all the restaurants, liquor stores, and bars. He just wanted to be alone. He needed to collect all the broken pieces of his marriage, examine them and try to put them back together. Just as he inserted the key into the back door, his phone buzzed; he was sure it was Ivy. But it wasn't. Disappointment chewed at his insides.

"Hey, Mom, how're the kids?" He had little energy to muster but took the steps to the fifth floor anyway.

"They are just fine, sweetie. How is she?"

"Not good. She made me leave. I've got some work to catch up on, so I will stay at the office and figure everything out Sunday. Are you still okay with keeping them until then?"

"Of course, sweetheart. I'm sorry that you and Ivy are going through this. Maybe she needs some space, and she'll feel better soon."

"I don't think so, Mom. I'm really worried about her. I think it might be over." Liam reached the fifth floor.

The line fell silent. Liam knew his mom had to feel and process things before she knew the right words to say to him. She would want to fix it, and she would want to save him. But his marriage and Ivy's confession of not loving him anymore was out of his mother's control, and out of his.

"I could talk to her, and we could…." She started with the saving, and Liam interrupted her, told her that he loved her promised to keep in touch until he saw her on Sunday. Then went to his office down the hall on the right, went inside, and closed the door behind him.

The quietness was deafening at first, but the thunder rolled, stealing the silence. He didn't mind. The light outside faded quickly. Liam closed his eyes and thought of Ivy and the last few months. It was bad, very bad. Maybe she was telling him the truth when she said she no longer loved him. She had grown distant and displeased with everything he did. He could barely breathe without her telling him that he was doing it too loudly or incorrectly. So, he's been holding his breath. And he's been holding it so long that he's grown weary.

Liam turns on his laptop, enters all his passwords, and stares at the screen. Who was he kidding? He can't focus enough to get any real work finished. He slams it shut and leans back in his chair. He hears something just as he grabs his suit jacket and truck keys. Nothing sinister or criminal, just normal workplace noise. Drawers are closing, heels tapping against the hardwood floor as someone walks around the front office area. He considered just hiding out in his office. The last thing he needed was anyone getting any ideas that he was sleeping at the office due to marital troubles. He would get a room when whoever was in the building left. Coming here had been a stupid idea. But it was too late; his office door swung open, and there she was. She nearly ran right into him, holding a stack of files in her arms. She screamed, and he reached out to assure her she was safe.

"Scarlett! It's just me, Liam!" He tried not to laugh as her face filled with terror.

"Liam! What the hell are you doing here?!" The tall woman dressed in a white pencil skirt suit, her strawberry blonde hair pulled into a tight bun at the nape of her neck, sighed with relief, and placed her hands on her chest as if she had just experienced a heart attack.

"Just taking care of some work stuff. You?" Liam noticed the files on the floor at their feet and kneeled to help pick them up.

"Same." She kneeled beside him to help gather the loose papers in a pile on the floor.

"I'm sorry I scared you. I heard you come in just as I was about to leave and didn't know how not to startle you.

"It's okay." The last paper was placed inside a manilla folder and closed. "I was just bringing you more work to do." She glanced at the files in her arms as they rose.

They noticed at the same time how close they were to one another. But neither attempted to move. Liam was looking at the tiny freckles spread across her nose. She was taken aback by his broad shoulders and the smell of his expensive aftershave.

Liam realized he was standing in her way and stepped aside. "You can just put those over on my desk. I'll pretend they aren't there until Monday morning."

Scarlett didn't say anything; she just did as she was told. Not that she took orders from Liam, as they are coworkers. He isn't her boss.

"Oh, here's your phone; you dropped it." He reached her phone out to her as she made her way back to his office door to leave. As she took her phone from his hand, she noticed something different. His wedding ring wasn't there on his finger as it always had been.

He felt her notice his bare left hand. "Yeah, it's been a rough night."

"I'm sorry about that." Her voice was low.

"Do you have any plans this evening? I could order takeout." He knew the words sounded desperate, but they had worked together for a year. They weren't strangers, and they were undoubtedly not unprofessional. They were just two coworkers alone on a Friday night.

"No, thank you." She replied, and Liam dropped his head with embarrassment and disappointment.

"Of course, you probably have a lot going on this weekend. I was just going to grab dinner and..."

Before he could finish, she interrupted him, "I'm not hungry," she whispered and took a step closer to him.

Before his heart started racing, it stopped for a brief second. Ironically, that's how long it took for him to decide yes or no. A brief second. Yes.

Her hand gently touched his face, letting his stubble tickle her palm. His lips reached hers. It was as if he had never wanted anything more. Ever. She tugged at his suit jacket. He unbuttoned her shirt as they backed further inside his office and over to the sofa. He didn't allow thoughts. He didn't let any voices whisper to him that he should stop. He did what felt right at this moment. She wanted him. Every bit of him. Finally, their clothes were on the floor. No more barriers existed between them. His skin was touching hers.

"Wait," she whispered. She removed Liam's hand from the side of her face and gazed at his lonely, indented ring finger. "Are you sure?" She searched his eyes, hoping his answer would be *yes*.

"I'm sure. I want you." He whispered, then placed his hand on her warm face and kissed those teasing little freckles on her nose.

It wasn't until sunrise on Sunday morning that he was no longer sure. Now he wasn't sure of anything. Scarlett lay next to him; her perfect naked body had stolen away all his pain and loneliness just as the storm had stolen the silence that early Friday evening. He wished he could close his eyes, and it would be Friday evening again. He felt sick. Liam quietly left the hotel bed, went to the bathroom, and closed the door. Everything was spinning around him as well as inside of him. He checked his phone, but there were only messages from his mother about the kids. Only once had Ivy tried to call him, but Liam's hands had been in Scarlett's hair, his mouth was caressing her breast, and he was falling apart. He had missed her call and ignored her voicemail until now. Now he wanted to hear Ivy's voice.

"I'm sorry, Liam. Please come home." That was it. That's all she said. That's all she needed to say. If he had listened to it or answered, it would have been enough for him to drive straight home. But he missed her call.

Chapter Eighteen

NOW

"I love you, Liam. Maybe I've loved you since that first night in your office. Am I crazy?" Her voice was low as they lay in the darkness, her body cuddled close to him, much like that Sunday morning long ago.

Liam doesn't want to say anything back, but the truth is he loves Scarlett in a small way. She isn't this magical thing at a rooftop bar on a rainy summer night, she isn't his wife, and she isn't the mother of his children. However, she is the woman who tried to make it all better; she is the woman who loves to be with him like this and outside of the bedroom. She was a broken, stormy Friday night and a warm hand in his after a long day. So yes, he does love her in small ways now.

"I love you too, Scar." It felt good to say it out loud. A few shattered pieces of him pulled back together and healed a little as he spoke the words to the woman in his bed, lying in his arms.

She rose, and his face met hers. Their eyes locked in the moonlight. Her body straddled his, and she pulled him close. It was so much more than a hug; it was other things, many things. It meant that after all this time, he was hers. All hers. They made love that night for the first time.

Afterward, Liam didn't think of Ivy. He let himself fall deeply asleep, and he would have probably slept until the alarm went off, but Scarlett whispered for him to wake up.

"What's wrong?" he rubbed his eyes to see the time on the alarm clock beside the bed.

"Your phone was vibrating. I think you have a missed call or message from someone." She handed him his phone.

"Thank you, baby." He took the phone but didn't recognize the number. He had five missed calls and two texts.

"What is it? Is everything okay?"

Liam read the text, "No, it's Joseph. Ivy is in the hospital. She had an accident."

The silence created a barrier between them. Scarlett could see his concern,

"You should go, make sure she's okay, and check on the kids."

He looked into her eyes and realized his "small love" for Scarlett didn't measure up to his feelings for his ex-wife. But maybe one day, that will change. Perhaps it would grow and take up more space in his heart.

He kissed her forehead, dressed, and sped away to Ivy, just like all the times before.

Once Liam parked in the parking garage, entered the hospital, and took the elevator up to the third floor, it was after midnight. He rushed to the nurse sitting at the nurse's station. It was dim and quiet.

"Can I help you?" The nurse with brown eyes looked tired.

"I'm looking for Ivy Cameron's room."

"Are you a relative?" This question had never surfaced before this moment. But it was pertinent. And difficult. He knows she won't let him see her if he says no. But it could get messy if he lies and says he's her husband. But he needs to see her; he needs to be with her.

"We have two kids together; she had a friend call me to come to see her. I'm her ex-husband." He searched her brown eyes for permission to pass by the desk and go down the long hall to Ivy's room. He could tell she was hesitant.

"Room 301. She's resting. Pretty severe head trauma. A concussion. Nothing too serious right now, but we are closely monitoring her. So far, she's stable."

Liam said thank you with a thankful smile and found her room down the hall. It smelled like band-aids. The door to room 301 was closed. Liam walked over to the window to look in before opening it. The nurse was right; Ivy was sleeping peacefully. Joseph was sitting in a chair with his head resting on her bed and her hand in his. Liam froze. He had been wrong to come. Joseph had texted everything the nurse said and that the kids were home with a sitter. She would take them to daycare in the morning. He wasn't needed. Ivy didn't need him anymore. She had Joseph. Liam stepped away from the glass and drove back home. He crept back into bed beside Scarlett. All those pieces she had seemed to mend earlier fell apart all over again.

Chapter Nineteen

NOW

"You get to go home today, Ms. Cameron." Ivy had been waiting to hear those words for two days. As the nurse reviewed home care instructions and restrictions, Ivy's mind wondered. She had only received one text a day from Liam since her accident. It usually went something like how are you feeling? The kids are doing well. That's it.

"You can call a family member to pick you up now, and once they arrive, we will wheel you down to patient pick in the front of the hospital. Ivy knows precisely where those sliding doors are located. She remembers Liam placing their babies in their car seats and then helping her inside. Sweet memories. Would she share those with her kids one day? Or would they only ever belong to her and Liam?

Her arm ached as she jokingly texted Joseph that she was ready to bust out of there. He messaged right back that he was on his way.

The wheelchair was uncomfortable, and the silence between the nurse and Ivy was awkward as they made their way down the sterile hospital elevators. Ivy never expected to lose her breath once she arrived at the sliding doors. She didn't lose it; something reached inside her and took it. The sunshine peeking through as people entered and others left, turned to darkness. The spring sounds changed to wind and rain. Her hands went numb, and she felt like she should stop the chair and run out into the storm. Faintly she could hear their cries, as well as Liam's. Her heart was racing as if she had really sprinted away.

"Ms. Cameron, are you okay? You don't look so good. Ms. Cameron?" The nurse touched her clammy skin and checked Ivy's pulse.

Then the cries faded, the rain stopped, and Ivy slipped away back into the dark corner where she was safe.

It was only seconds until she came to. Joseph had made it inside and was next to the nurse comforting her. Another nurse was taking her blood pressure. Stares and gasps were all around her. She could feel them burning into her skin.

"I'm okay. I promise. I think I just got a little overwhelmed, and my leg hurts badly."

"She was instructed to have someone be with her for a day or two, especially while she is on the pain medications." The nurse with blonde curls rested her hand on Joseph's shoulder.

"I'll stay with her. She will be fine." Liam moved away from the nurse's touch and assisted with the wheelchair. His truck was parked just outside those horrid doors. She tried so hard to will the cries to stay behind as the doors closed behind them. But she knew that was impossible; those screams were etched inside her soul. They would go with her to her grave. No one or nothing could silence the sounds of children's cries of pain.

Chapter Twenty

NOW

Scarlett's heart turns to mush as little fingers wrap around her own. She holds the sweet little girl close in the oversized recliner, the soft blanket covering them as they watch the princess run barefoot across the kingdom after the little white bunny who stole her crown on the television.

The last few days have been like a dream, and she never wants to wake up. She could stay right here in this little home sleeping next to Liam at night and taking care of the kids during the day. She has learned so much about them already. She knows Kimber only drinks from straw sippy cups and prefers apple juice, but she loves water. Kimber is fragile and delicate, and she really loves her mom. Scarlett can tell, as they snuggle watching television or while she is rocking her to sleep at night, Kimber turns around often, looking to see if it's her mama whose arms she is being held by, and Scarlett can see the disappointment in those eyes every time she realizes it's not.

Benjamin is the opposite of fragile and delicate. He's all boy. He always runs, pushes a little metal car over the coffee table, or jumps from the couch to the loveseat. Liam tells him not to, but she lets him do it. He's so much like Liam. From his eyes to the way he tilts his head to the right just a little when he's watching or listening to something intently.

The front door opens, Liam steps inside, and the moment ends. The kids have warmed up to her, but their dad hangs the moon.

She watches as he rests his brown leather briefcase on the hardwood floor and kneels so the little girl and boy can run into his arms. He then hugs them tight and tickles their little tummies until they can't laugh anymore.

Once Ben scurries away to find his new little green tractor, and Kimber rests her head on her dad's shoulder, he walks over to Scarlett, leans down, and gently kisses her lips. Her insides melt all over again. This is everything she has wanted for so long. And she plans to keep it just like this for as long as she can.

"Who wants to go out for pizza?" Liam spoke the magic word.

"Me! Me, Daddy, me! I want to get pizza!" The little boy with his dad's dark curly hair and brown eyes jumps up and down with his tractor in his hand.

"I'll take the baby girl and get her ready." Scarlett rises and holds out her hands to Liam's daughter. They both watch as Kimber looks at her dad and then back to the woman who has been caring for her these past few days. Her little hands unlatch from her father's suit jacket, and she leans toward her. Elated with joy, Scarlett pulls her close, wishing the little girl in the pink outfit with hearts on it was hers.

Chapter Twenty-One

NOW

"Easy, take your time. We don't want you passing out again."

Ivy's head spins as they enter her bedroom. The house is silent. She can hear the clock down the hall. Tick. Tock. Tick. Tock. She misses her kids. She misses Liam.

Joseph pulls back the covers, and Ivy lies down. "This feels like heaven compared to the hospital bed. Thank you, Joseph. For everything."

"I'll get you some water and then make dinner. Any requests?" Joseph pulled the cream duvet up to her chest.

"Actually, I'm not hungry. I want to sleep and have Liam bring the kids home tomorrow. But thank you, Joseph. So much."

"Are you sure?" Disappointment spread across his face. But there was little Ivy cared to do about it.

"I'm sure. I have my meds and my phone. I'm good. I'll call you if I change my mind. Promise."

"I could always stay, and we could watch a movie. You can rest, and I'll just be here in case you need anything."

Ivy grew annoyed and impatient. "I said I'm good." She let out a sigh and closed her eyes.

"Okay, then." Joseph left the room, returning moments later with a bottle of water, and placed it on her bedside table. "I'll bring breakfast and coffee in the morning and…"

"That's okay. I can make myself something. Don't miss work. I'll call you."

She didn't need to open her eyes this time to see the disappointment across his face; she could feel it. It was loud in the silence between them.

"Thank you again, Joseph. I just need a little time." She whispered.

"I understand. I'll lock up on my way out." He whispered back.

In a blink, he was gone, and she could hear the front door lock turning.

It isn't that she doesn't like Joseph. He's very kind, intelligent, attractive and present. The only problem is that he isn't Liam. She just isn't ready. She will be one day. But not today.

Chapter Twenty-Two

Fear has a way of stealing the most precious things from us. It comes in the night, long after the sun has set and the bedside lamp has been switched off. It comes into the room alongside the sunlight, bright and early in the morning. Fear slithers in and wraps around your whole being sometimes. And you're just stuck. For days. And nights. It becomes harder and harder to breathe, and then one day, that fear lets go little by little, without you even noticing. Time passes, and all the things that were taken are returned. They're different, very different. But much the same. Laughter, joy, hope, excitement… all things gone yesterday and somehow back today. So much so that your perspective is comparing yesterday to today over everything. You can barely believe it. The lesson was impossible, and the loss was immeasurable, but once you let go and let something new in, fear loses, and the new you, the "I know better now" you, wins.

Liam never thought he could feel like this again. He thought he would live a life of Sundays. But here they are, something as simple as sitting in the booth side by side. Scarlett carefully slices the pizza and helps Kimber as she sits in the wooden highchair. "Here comes the airplane!" Scarlett moves the fork through the air as if passing through the clouds in the sky to the little one's mouth. Laughter bursts from Ben as he arm wrestles his dad and wins. Liam can't help but notice that Scarlett is glowing. She's a natural, he thinks. He rests his hand on hers, and she looks up at him. "Thank you." He hesitates, but he can't hold back. He has to say it. For him. And for her. "I love you." He mouths. And he means it. He watches the tears fill her eyes, and he squeezes her hand. " I love you too, Liam." She mouths back silently.

This was the part that fear had taken. After his marriage was over, he came to know pretty quickly that there was a reason it was Scarlett who he called on the difficult days; it was Scarlett whose arms he crawled into at night. It was Scarlett… that he had fallen in love with. Scarlett didn't steal him. He quit. Quit on his wife, on his family. And then he had to live with that. He never expected this or thought he deserved any of it.

Who knew happiness could be found sitting in a booth at a pizza pub? Liam thought as he watched a new version of his family make a memory.

But all good things must come to an end. Liam's gut wrenched as he read the message from his ex-wife asking him to bring the kids home. It had been a good test run.

He had always wondered if Scarlett would be a good bonus mom and if the kids would accept her. Fear kept him from hoping both were possible. Now he knows they are.

Chapter Twenty-Three

THEN

How much could God cry? Liam wondered as he stared out the streaked hotel window from the bed on the twentieth floor. The rain had refused to slow since the moment he took Scarlett into his arms that very first night. He knew the raindrops didn't compare to the tears of disappointment and sadness God must feel because of him. The woman lying in his arms suddenly felt more like a morning hangover headache instead of the cure to all his pain these past two nights. Her warmth had been like swallowing a magic pill that chased away a disease. Her company is much like a cold drink after a long run on a sweltering, hot summer day. This morning as the sun rises, she feels more like an intense, almost unbearable pain. His mouth was dry, and the room had grown smaller. The heat was causing his armpits to itch as the moisture collected. Little did he know that he traded his marriage and family for a placebo.

He hoped a shower would fix him as he washed her away. Everything became crystal clear. Forty-eight hours ago, his marriage was rocky. Now it was lava. There would be no coming back from this, not in Ivy's heart nor his own.

There was a slight tap at the bathroom door. Moments later, the foreign tall curvy woman with strawberry blonde hair stepped beneath the rain shower stream and into his arms. He rested his forehead down onto hers.

"Oh God, Scar. What have I done?" His gut wrenched; jagged steel knives punctured him from the inside out. He was drowning beneath that warm shower holding on to Scarlett for dear life like a lifeboat. But it's the lifeboat that will ultimately sink him.

Chapter Twenty-Four

THEN

"I'm sure he was at the office all weekend getting caught up with work, Ivy. I mean, he's been going through this postpartum depression right alongside you. He's exhausted." Liam's mother stood with her hands on her hips in the doorway of her massive red brick home. Her thinning gray hair was not as tidy as usual. The kids must have kept her on her toes all weekend; Ivy thought as anger choked her. But she swallowed hard as she carried the bags to the car. The relentless downpour of rain was drenching her hair and clothes. She had already buckled the kids into their car seats.

But then there it was. She regurgitated the anger. It was expelling, and there was nothing she could do about it.

She slammed her driver's door shut and nearly ran back to her mother-in-law, still perched on her high horse.

"Melanie, you have no idea what this feels like. You haven't a clue how hard I have tried to save myself. Yes, Liam is the best husband and father, and he's tired, and we are not in a good place. But I am trying to keep my head above water, and what have you done besides criticize me? You've certainly done nothing to help! Screw you, Melanie."

Headlights pulled into the drive, and Ivy instantly knew it was Liam. Relief flooded her. She needed him. He was finally here, like a knight in shining armor.

The truck jolted to a stop. He didn't take the time to turn off the windshield wipers or the headlights.

"Liam!" Ivy ran into his open arms, and all was right in the world again. "I'm so sorry. I should never have told you to leave. I'm going to do better. I promise."

He stepped back, and Ivy looked into his eyes as the rain poured down on them. "I promise." She whispered as she pulled him back.

"I messed up, Ivy."

A chill ran down her spine; all her extremities suddenly shook, and her cheeks burned. She looked deeper into his eyes, and there it was. He needn't use words. His eyes told her everything. The same eyes that told her that he would love her forever in that summer rain years ago. Those eyes were liars.

She stepped backward while shaking her head back and forth, saying, "No." The sound was more like a mumble under her breath, but she wasn't speaking it to him. She was talking to the universe, to God.

Liam stepped toward her as she backed away. Her head moved back and forth fiercely. He went to pull her close.

"No!" she screamed with everything inside of her. "No! You don't touch me!" She could see that he was crying, and so was she. Tears mixed with the rain on her face.

"Please, Ivy. I'm so sorry!"

The world was spinning. She couldn't breathe. The moon had found a place to hide because the darkness invaded the night, making it impossible to see anything as she jumped inside her car and locked the doors. Without thinking, she threw the car in reverse and sped away. She drove for seconds before realizing she needed to turn on her windshield wipers. But there was nothing she could use to wipe away the flashes. The subdivision was never-ending. Should she turn right or left? Where was she? Flashes of his hands in a woman's hair. She covered her mouth so as not to cry out. Right, she goes right to get back home from here. She turned on her right turn signal. Then a flash of his lips on someone else's. She covered her eyes and bit down on her tongue. It was clear; she pulled out onto the main road and sped up. Flashes of him breathing in someone else, feeling her, inside out. Her foot pressed the gas pedal harder. Doom was taking her, and she was going to let it. As the car sped toward the large tree, she didn't scream as she watched it get closer by millisecond. But her babies in the back did.

Chapter Twenty-Five

NOW

"Do you want to ride with us, Scarlett? You can sit in the backseat with Kimby and me." Liam watched as Scarlett pulled Ben close.

"I definitely will next time, buddy. Okay? I need to do a little work this evening before bed. But I will see you this Friday, promise."

"Okie dokie." He hugged her neck, then ran off to Liam's truck.

"I'll see you Friday as well, little munchkin." Kimber giggled as Scarlett tickled her tummy.

Liam had no idea how to manage the kids alone while Ivy was recovering. But Scarlett had offered, and now everything was different, in a good way. The hardest part would be telling Ivy about this. They had agreed to talk before they let the kids meet "someone new." But this situation left him no choice as his mother had moved to Colorado months ago.

"I'll call you as soon as I drop them off?" He entangled Scar's hand with his.

"We have some one-on-one time to catch up on. So, you better hurry." Scarlett bit her lower lip and gave him a sly grin.

"I'll be back in two shakes."

It wasn't until he was at his old front door and heard Holden barking that he felt a ping of guilt. He gave a few knocks and then stepped inside.

"Mama!" Ben dashed for his mom, coming down the hall and into the foyer. The little girl in his arms wrestled to get down and walked preciously toward her as well.

"My sweet babies. Come here and let me see you!" She hugged and kissed their little faces.

Liam didn't move from the front door. Holden was lying on his back as Liam patted his belly.

"I'll go get their things." It was the first time he had seen her since her accident. Her face was bruised, and she was limping. Liam's first instinct was to help her, to fix her. But he refrained. He looked away as the kids touched her boo-boos, and she told them she would be okay.

He sat the bags inside the door. "Come give me a hug, kiddos. Dad's got to go." He pulled them in and hugged them tight. He wished they were with him every day. He rose and opened the door, "Goodnight, Ivy. Let me know if you need anything." He needed to run.

"Liam, wait." Ivy put the baby in her playpen as Ben took off to his room with his tractor.

"How did everything go this week? I'm really sorry. It's so crazy." Liam could smell Ivy from a mile away. She smelled the same as she did when he asked her to marry him. But now it's different. It doesn't hurt so bad anymore to smell her. Vanilla. Soap. Joy. Those are the ingredients to Ivy's aroma—his favorite things.

"It was good. No worries. I'm just happy you're okay." Liam didn't step back into the house. One foot was out the door, and one was in. Holden went back to his water bowl in the kitchen.

Ivy stepped closer. Her long dark hair spilled onto her cleavage. What was she doing? Was she flirting with him?

"I am okay. Between Joseph and Tia, I've been well taken care of."

Liam hesitated, but he could tell she was hurt by his staying away. "I'm glad they were here for you. Listen, I've got to run." He needed to go. He needed to get back to Scarlett, who was waiting on him.

"Stay." Her hand rested on his cheek. Her eyes were inches away now, staring into his. He froze. Then there was the familiar feeling of her full lips on his. Strangely, it felt wrong. As wrong as everything that felt right moments ago when he kissed Scar in the driveway. This was everything he had begged God for over and over for months. For her to want him again. All of him.

Liam pulled away. He stepped back, and now both feet were outside of the house they once shared. "I can't," he whispered and tried to look away, "We'll talk tomorrow."

"Is there someone else? Have you met someone?" The bruises on her face were turning green. The scrapes were fading. But the sadness in her eyes hurt him just as badly as her fall had hurt her days ago.

"I didn't want to do this right now. You've been through a lot and..."

Ivy watched Liam run his hand through his dark curly hair like she had seen him do a thousand times before. "Liam, it's okay. Look at me." She pulled at his hand and covered it with her own. Her skin was as soft as the first time she danced with him.

"I'm sorry. I just..." his voice cracked, and he looked down, "I just don't want to hurt you."

"I'm okay. I'm better than I was that night in your mother's driveway. I can handle it; you deserve to be happy. When we divorced, I knew you would make someone else very happy one day."

Tears slid down her cheeks, and she knew she was right. There was someone else. And he knew she was telling the truth; she was better. She could be sad, but deal with it—even this.

"It's her, Ivy. It's Scarlett. She stays with me most of the time and helped me with the kids this week. I hope that's okay. I really didn't have a choice." The space between them was full of despair and pain. "I'm in love with her." Liam expected fireworks. He expected fire. But Ivy just wiped her tears away and took a deep breath.

She pulled him close one last time. She held on to him like she did when she told him she loved him for the first time, and now this would be the last time. She whispered,

"I'm happy for you." She gently kissed his cheek, turned, walked back inside, and closed the door.

Chapter Twenty-Six

NOW

The world didn't stop spinning. The hand on the clock down the hall didn't stop ticking, and her heart hadn't given up. It was still beating. Ivy had lied. She hadn't seen Joseph since he brought her home from the hospital, and Tia was out of town taking care of her mother. She had spent her days and nights getting better alone. And she was better.

Ivy sat the fogged wine glass down on the edge of the tub and then leaned back into the hot, steamy water. Her body still hurt, but nothing like the days after her fall. And nothing hurt like her chest. She kept replaying those words over and over. *"I'm in love with her."* He was hurting when he said them; she will give him credit for that. Her phone buzzed across the room on the counter near the sink. Liam may be ready to love someone again, but she was not. Maybe one day, but not tonight.

Later, after she wrapped her favorite white robe around her body, she turned off all the lights, checked in on her babies one last time, and then crawled into her bed. When she had made it this morning, she had expected that the next time she ran her skin over the smooth sheets, it would be with Liam's arms around her. But she was too late. She would accept it; she had no choice. She had already lost him a long time ago. And then, the parts that remained after he did what he did, she lost them piece by piece over time until there was nothing but pain and disappointment. And that's what tonight would have been. More shattered fragments of a broken life she had already swept up with a broom and thrown away.

Just as her weary eyes drifted to sleep, something startled her. But as she looked around the room, she wondered what. Then she heard footsteps coming up the stairs quietly. It was impossible to see in the dark. Was it Liam? Was it an intruder? She froze, like Liam, when she kissed him tonight on her doorstep.

The doorknob to her bedroom turned, and the door slowly crept open.

Ivy's heart was pounding so loudly she could barely hear Tia's voice say her name. "Oh, Ivy. Come here."

Ivy hadn't cried when Liam didn't come to her after she fell at the cabin or when he didn't visit her in the hospital with the kids, and he never came to check on her once she was home. She didn't ugly cry after he told her he loved the woman who stole his body from her that rainy weekend in the same city he met Ivy in. But she was bursting into tears now. Tia was a safe place. She's the best friend form of what Liam once was.

"Cry it out, babe. Let it out."

She rocked back and forth as she held Ivy close while she sobbed, hoping they didn't wake the children fast asleep in their beds.

It was as if she had truly cried him away this time. She had nothing left. No love for Liam, nor any other man…for now.

"Wait, did you drive all this way just because I texted you about what an idiot I am?" Ivy wiped her eyes.

"Of course I did. My best friend is not an idiot. She just loves too much."

Her hand rubbed up and down Ivy's back as she let out a long sigh of relief.

"How could it be her? She wins." Ivy bites at her bottom lip.

"She didn't win. No one won. The game's over. It has been for a long time. Now it's time to play a different game. With a different team."

"You're right," Ivy whispered. The two friends lay on the soft mattress and pulled the cover over them as they held on tight. Scared to let go.

"Thank you for coming to be with me, Tia."

"That's what book club members do you know? They laughed as Ivy's heart slowed and the calmness in her soul returned.

Chapter Twenty-Seven

NOW

Liam's hands shook. He grasped the steering wheel a little tighter. But it didn't help. The last time he told Ivy something painful, she lost herself. He broke her when she was already breaking. And in one moment, he almost lost his kids too. He could still hear their cries as he ran to them in the pouring rain. They were awake and okay, but Ivy wasn't. Even when she opened her eyes in the hospital, she wasn't okay. Liam was terrified the same reaction would replay once he spoke even more painful words to her again. But it didn't. Ivy was hurt, but she stood strong. She had already weathered a lot; Liam knew this was what she had feared most all along. Loving Scarlett was everything Ivy never wanted to happen, but here they are. He loved her, and he hadn't lied.

He didn't waste any time. He knew Scar was home, worried. Not doing work stuff like she had told his son earlier. He found her on the sofa, wrapped in a throw from the back of his couch. A muted documentary about a serial killer played on television.

Liam removed his shoes, found his place beside her, and sighed.

"Hey." She whispered in the dark.

"Hey." He tucked a strand of strawberry curls behind her ear.

"How did that go?" she asked.

"Better than expected."

"Did you want to stay with her?" He could hear the sadness in her whisper this time.

"No. I wanted to get back home to you."

"Promise?" She asked with pouty lips.

"Swear." He pulled her closer, and she straddled his lap.

She smiled and touched her lips to his. "Did you kiss her?"

Liam froze as hard as he had when Ivy's lips touched his moments ago.

He didn't know what to say. So, he told the truth. "Ivy kissed me. She asked me to stay. And that's when I told her that you met the kids and that… that I love you."

Her suspicious eyes met his, searching for the truth in his words.

"Move in with me. Be here with me. Me and the kids. If you want to, I mean," Liam asked excitedly.

Her chest paused as she allowed tears to fill her eyes. "Yes." She smiled, and he smiled bigger.

Liam thought that life has a way of correcting itself when you want it to, as his mouth covered hers.

Just as her clothes were on the floor, as her tongue slid up his neck, and he felt all of her all around him, she whispered something into his ear, and she didn't stutter, and her voice didn't crack. He heard her whisper loud and clear.

"If you ever hurt me…I will hate you. Forever."

He did more than hear her; he understood her.

Chapter Twenty-Eight

NOW

"Who wants pancakes?!" She could hear Ben coming down the hall as fast as he could, shouting, "Me!"

"I know you want pancakes, little miss Sugarplum." Ivy kissed the top of her daughter's head. She smelled like strawberries and crème.

Loving Liam was one thing, but Scarlett loving her children was something very different, she thought as she slowly spread butter over Ben's pancake. She lost pieces of Liam over incriminates of time. Now was she just supposed to hand over half of her children to her, just like that? She wouldn't. Not yet. She needs more time. More time to let go a little.

Only her hands had held onto theirs as they slept in her arms. Only her breasts had nursed them when they were born. Only her warm hugs had comforted them when they cried. And now, she would have to share them with someone she had never even seen. But Liam has chosen her. The woman he turned to when their marriage was crumbling will be the woman who gets all the things she dreamt of from the first time she looked into his eyes that rainy summer night. She gets his laughter, his touch, and his protection. She also gets to be by his side during their children's birthdays, graduations, weddings, and so on. She gets to grow old with him. She gets all the moments.

"May I have more syrup, mama?" Ben's fingers are already sticky, but he doesn't seem to mind.

"Of course, you may, buddy; I'll pour it for you." Ivy drizzled more maple syrup over his half-eaten pancake with blueberries on top.

"I was at Daddy's house, he made us pancakes, and when Scarlett poured my syrup, she let me help her. I was a big boy. Not a baby."

Well, it was already starting. Her role as her children's queen was diminishing. It's not a competition, but it is. And Ivy hates it.

"I'm so proud of you; next time we have pancakes, I'll let you help me, okay, buddy?"

"Okay, Mama."

Ivy willed herself not to cry. "Mama, I think your pancakes are the best in the world."

"That's so nice, Ben. Thank you."

Ivy swiped a tear away as she cut up her daughter's pancake and offered some to Kimber, who made a face, pulled the pancake from her mouth with her fingers, and threw it onto the tiled floor. Kimber obviously didn't feel the same about her mama's pancakes as her older brother. Ivy chuckled and kissed the little angel's cheek. "Here you go, kiddo. Try this." Ivy handed her an on-the-go applesauce pack, and Kimber approved. Ivy knew this because Kimber didn't throw the package to the floor until it was all gone.

Later that evening, Ivy was ecstatic when she noticed her best friend walking up the sidewalk. Ivy met her at the front door. "Tia! Thank God!"

"I brought books and goodies!" Tia held up several bags from the bookstore and local coffee shop. Ivy could smell the aroma of her vanilla latte and Tia's caramel cappuccino.

"You are my favorite book club member!" Ivy helped with the drinks, and they sat on the front porch swing. Spring had led into summer a long time ago in North Carolina. Sitting on the front porch as the sun goes down can be sticky, but this evening is perfect.

"I'm the only member besides you, but I'll take it." Tia joked as she tucked a long blond curl behind her ear.

A familiar annoying voice came from the sidewalk in front of the house. "Hey, neighbor! It's good to see you are out and about again. I heard about your little accident." Ivy couldn't help but roll her eyes and then look at Tia.

She could tell by Tia's face that she quickly realized who the woman was.

"Thank you, Brandy. I'm happy to back up on two feet."

"You know, it wouldn't kill you to join me for a run every now and then. It would be good for you." Ivy's neighbor wearing black leggings with a matching black sleeveless top, stretched her legs one by one against a tree.

"Actually, it would kill me," Ivy whispered to Tia, and she laughed.

"What was that?" Brandy asked, pausing to hear Ivy sitting on the swing.

"I will definitely do that soon. I'll text you." Ivy lied.

Brandy threw her a wave and was gone jogging down the street.

"She is the worst." Tia took a sip of coffee.

"Right?!"

"So, what final book did you choose for us?" Ivy sipped on her warm drink and sat back.

"Oh, just a little book called Tia's Not Moving Away From Her Best Friend Ever."

Ivy sat straight, swallowed her mouthful of hot brew, and smiled big. "You're joking?!"

"Nope. My mom was admitted to the Hospice unit yesterday, and I broke up with what's his name. So, I'm staying." Tia removed a hair tie from her wrist, then pulled her long blonde curly hair into a high ponytail.

"I'm sorry, Tia. I know you were ready for bigger, better things."

"You need me too much, and besides, you'd be pathetic running this book club all on your own."

The sun sunk deeper into the earth, taking the light with it as it whispered goodbye. Whatever bad feelings that had wandered inside Ivy's heart today had been banished somewhere far away. Tia has a way of doing that; she enters the room, and the weariness feels less, hope enters, and breathing is easier. Ivy knew Tia was right; she does need her too much for her to go right now. So, she will keep her close until she doesn't need her help to breathe anymore.

Chapter Twenty-Nine

NOW

"Why are we not going to see Daddy and Scarlett, Mommy?" Ben pretended that the dinosaur in his left hand with big teeth and small arms was eating the dinosaur with a long neck in his right hand.

"Your dad just said he had to take care of something important today, sweetie. But he will be coming to get you this evening." Ivy tied Kimber's shoelaces and kissed her on the top of her head.

There was a tap on the front door, and then it opened. Ivy smiled as Joseph walked in. Ben and Kimber had already made their way into the living room as she finished slipping into her brown laced sandals. Their plans to spend the weekend away turned into a date to the Farmers Market with the kiddos and then maybe a quiet dinner lakeside. The day was beautiful, and they didn't want to waste a minute.

"Hey." Joseph closed the door behind him as Ivy rose to her feet.

"Hey." She only looked into his sexy eyes briefly before his lips touched hers. His tongue filled her mouth, and his warm, steady hand touched her cheek. She couldn't remember if she had stood because she felt like she was floating.

Her body ached for him. The closer he pulled her into him, the deeper she breathed in and out. Then his kiss turned tender. His hand moved from her cheek to her hand, and then her feet returned to the floor. Whatever Liam had to do today better be very important for her to cancel their weekend away.

"I really enjoy your *hellos*." Her cheeks remained flushed for most of the drive to town.

As they strolled through the crowd of familiar faces and some unfamiliar ones, the four of them may have slightly resembled a family—a happy one. One of Ivy's hands held onto her sons, and Joseph held her other gently. A little girl with light brown curls bounced on his shoulders as they made their way through all the vendors.

The sound of live folksy music played nearby. Ivy's heart swayed to the strum of the guitar. The smell of fresh barbeque cooking over hot charcoal made her mouth water. But what she really wanted, no needed, was a coffee.

"I have an idea! Why don't Joseph and I get coffees, and we will get you two some berry smoothies? Does that sound nice?"

Ben jumped up and down with approval as they made their way to the coffee shop. Joseph looked happy, Ivy noticed this, and her heart skipped a beat but fixed itself. She didn't want to hurt him. She had been very honest about her heart. She was still hurting and healing. He had agreed to be patient and understanding. They would take things slow. But after that kiss this morning, Ivy wasn't so sure she didn't want to speed things up a bit.

The tall, dark blonde man holding her hand must have been able to read her mind because when she looked up at him, their eyes met. He gave her a wink, then leaned down to kiss her as they walked. There goes her heart again, skipping beats and dancing to that guitar.

"Ivy?" She was still gleaming when she heard her name. The pseudo-family of four stopped on the street in unison.

"Daddy! Daddy!" Ben dropped his mother's hand and ran into his father's arms. Ivy didn't let go of Joseph's. In fact, she gave it a squeeze.

"Hey buddy, what are you up to this morning?" Liam's eyes darted to his ex-wife and then to the man whose lips were just on hers. His cheeks were flushed, but for a different reason than why Ivy's was earlier.

"We are getting smoothies. Right, mama?!"

A sweet voice coming from the little girl on Joseph's shoulders said *Da Da* and held out her arms. Joseph helped her down and handed her to her father.

"There's my baby girl."

Ivy was still holding Joseph's hand. Maybe it was because he felt more like home to her; perhaps it was because she felt uncomfortable being this close to a man in front of her ex-husband, whom she still had feelings for and probably always would. But her best guess was because she didn't want to fall. Her knees were weak; her heart wasn't skipping beats;

it was trying not to stop altogether. She needed him to keep her from falling because she was looking at the woman with strawberry blonde hair standing close to Liam.

This woman wasn't some date or someone he had just recently met and was getting serious with. This woman was the person who held Liam when he was still Ivy's. This woman had taken her favorite thing in the whole world from her, and she was never giving it back. This woman would probably be the woman she will have to share birthdays and holidays with. But Ivy noticed the woman wasn't particularly "happy" to see Liam's children. She wasn't secure and comfortable at this moment. She appeared to be threatened by Ivy and looked as if she might try to grab Liam and run back to that hotel in Charlotte.

"I'm sorry. Um, Ivy, Joseph, this is Scarlett." Liam looked as if he might vomit. He was green, like the color of pond scum.

Ivy, still not letting go of Joseph's hand, reached out her other one and offered it to the woman who woke up in Liam's arms this morning.

"Hi, Scarlett. It's nice to meet you." To Ivy's surprise, her voice sounded steady, even though her soul shook.

Scarlett hesitated. She looked at Ivy as if she were a bug she'd like to squash and just might if she ever had the opportunity. But then, the tall curvy woman wearing a black cover-up over her black bikini and a large bag over her shoulder with towels peeking out the top extended her hand and took Ivy's. As soon as their skin touched, it was like fire. So cold Ivy's fingertips burned.

"Pleasure." She offered Ivy a smile and then Joseph. "Liam, baby, if we are going to make it to the dock by noon, we must go soon. Nick already has the boat gassed up and ready."

Liam's eyes grew wide, and fury filled Ivy's.

"Hi, sweet babies. I have missed you both so much. Come here." Scarlett kneeled in her super short, thin, off-the-shoulder cover-up and squeezed both kids. Ben petted her hair as she told them they would make burgers on the grill and watch a movie on a big screen outside this evening. Kimber's little fingers gripped the skin on the back of her arm, smiling endearingly at the new woman who magically came into this fairy tale to love them like an actual princess. Joseph had pulled Ivy close and was rubbing her bare shoulder. Suddenly she felt vulnerable, like a prude in her khaki shorts and loose-fitting pale blue tank top.

"You guys run along with your mama, and I'll see you soon, okay."

"But, can you take us with you on the boat? I'll go get all my stuff from Joseph's truck!"

"Not right now, Ben, but I'll see you tonight. Okay?" Liam stood, and Scarlett wrapped both arms around his left one. He was hers now, and she was making sure everyone in town, especially Ivy, knew it.

Ivy and Joseph reminded Ben of their smoothies and maybe even a hot dog with ketchup, then all was better as the couples parted ways.

"You did great," Joseph whispered into her ear, then kissed her forehead. And just like that, her heart was skipping again.

Chapter Thirty

NOW

The air was thick, and the breeze felt like an answered prayer. Just outside Charlotte, North Carolina, it feels like the ocean is nearby, but it's not. It's the strangest thing. But a lake is just up the road, and a black cabin cruiser is waiting at the dock, ready to be fired up.

But no matter how hot the weather was, the air between Liam and Scarlett in his truck was hotter. In fact, Liam was steaming.

"I don't understand why you are so angry." Scarlett's arms crossed her chest as she stared out the window.

"You were rude. You didn't even try to be friendly to Ivy. Not to mention, you brought up the boat today. It looked like we were taking the boat out for a joy ride and not to meet a possible buyer."

Silence mixed with the humidity. Strawberry-colored flyaways of hair danced in the wind as the truck sped down the curvy road to Lake Morissette.

Scarlett knew if she parted her lips to speak, she would cry. And she wasn't about to look weak to the man she had fallen so desperately in love with. He was finally all hers, and she wanted to keep him. Scar noticed how Liam's back grew straight, his arms tensed, and his breathing grew deep when he saw Ivy. She could sense the jealousy pouring out of him as he tried not to acknowledge the tall, athletic, attractive man who carried Liam's daughter on his shoulders and held his ex-wife's hand in his. Scar could practically feel Liam's heart racing and breaking all at once. And she hated it. It hurt. She wanted to mean more to him than Ivy. She wanted to be the person who took up the space in his heart that Ivy left vacant.

It wasn't until Liam parked the truck in his designated parking spot and covered his face with his hands that Scarlett started to speak.

"I'm sorry. I just..."

"No, Scar. It's okay," Liam interrupted, "I'm an ass. I know this is hard for you. It's hard for me." He took a deep breath and kissed her. His hands were sweaty, but he tangled them in her wild hair anyway.

"Come with me." He whispered.

Scarlett liked how he took her hand and led her down to the dock and across the way to the cabin cruiser, whose motor was already humming like a dream. The boards under their feet creaked as they walked quickly to his boat. Liam stepped aboard first and then held out his hand to help the woman in the black bikini.

Liam did all the things necessary to free the boat from the dock. Scarlett watched as he maneuvered around as if he'd done it a million times. And he probably had. But never with her. She hated to sell the boat. But it had been Liam and Ivy's, so it needed to go, along with everything else that put their names side by side.

"Where are we going?" Scarlett sat as the boat sped away much too fast for a NO WAKE ZONE, the sign was large, and Liam knew it was there but obviously didn't care.

"We don't have much time."

Liam's shirt was wet with sweat. He pulled it over his head, tucked it inside the glove box, then placed his baseball cap backward. Little wisps of dark hair peeked out on the sides and back. He had said a few days ago he needed a haircut, but Scarlett didn't think so.

They were hidden in a cove within a few minutes, the engine calmed, and the anchors were dropped.

"What now?" Scarlett looked around and took in the quiet sounds of nature. They were practically invisible from the wide-open lake. She heard a fish jump nearby, but only a ripple on top of the green-blue water was left behind when she looked.

"Come with me." Liam gave her a wink and took her hand. She let him take her through a small door and down into the cabin. The air had been running, so it was inviting. She could finally breathe. The heat had been strangling her. Ever since that dreaded moment, she let Ivy take her hand in hers.

The area was large, and everything was shiny and new. Only small bouts of sunlight trying to peek through the blinds shed light down below.

"Come here." Liam led Scarlett over to the bed. The navy blue comforter was cool and soft against the back of her thighs as she sat. Liam gently pulled her cover-up over her head as she held her arms up in the air. She tugged at his solid gray swimming trunks until they were beside him on the floor. She removed his ball cap and tossed it aside. It fell onto the floor beside the bed. Her fingertips got lost in his soft dark hair as he loved her gently but with all of his heart. He loved her; she could tell. He was hurting, and she made it better like always. But now, he touched, kissed, and felt of her in ways that meant something more than those first hundred times they were together.

"I love you so damn much." Liam professed.

Scarlett was breathing too hard to reply. But the words were there; the love was there, now and in the moments after.

As they dozed in one another's arms, the boat slowly rocked back and forth, putting them to sleep like a lullaby.

"Will we be late meeting Mr. Burns?" Scarlett's mouth was dry.

"I don't care," Liam mumbled as he pulled the covers over their bare bodies. "I just want to do this all day. Over and over."

Scarlett didn't protest. She let his warm mouth kiss her skin.

And then Joseph can buy this damn thing, Liam thought as he tasted every inch of Scarlett's body one more time as he tried to force the image of Joseph with his wife and family on the street earlier, like a happy little family.

Chapter Thirty-One

NOW

Right on time, Liam's truck pulled into the drive. He had to park behind Joseph. This made Ivy smile. She peeked through the blinds of the laundry room window and watched Liam do something she had never seen him do before. He kissed another woman. He did it like he does when he's happy, fulfilled, and had sex. Ivy took a deep breath. *Serves you right for spying,* she scolded herself as she gathered the kids; their bags were already near the front door.

The doorbell rang as she once again tied Kimber's laces. She heard Joseph tell Liam that she would be right down. That's awkward, but what can you do? She was trying to hurry.

Ivy couldn't help but notice how handsome Joseph looked as she came down the stairs. He was a little taller than Liam, leaner, and more confident. She also couldn't help but notice that Liam looked exhausted and sunburnt. "Have a nice day on the lake, Liam?" Ivy handed him their daughter.

"We were meeting a prospective buyer, Ivy. Not taking the boat for a joyride." Liam tensed.

"Really, and how did that go?" She was being sarcastic, but she didn't care. She was supposed to be having her own joyride.

"He never showed." He then turned to Joseph. "If you're still interested…she's all yours."

Ivy wasn't sure if Liam was talking about their boat or her until he reached the keys on the floating yellow keychain out to Joseph. She had picked out that keychain at the marina the first day they took her out. Ivy stopped breathing. She knew that Liam meant both their boat and her. He was letting them both go for real this time.

"Thank you, maybe Ivy and I will take her for a spin tomorrow." He took the keys from Liam, and Liam offered a tired smile.

"Enjoy." Liam rounded up the kids and their things, dumped all the baggage from their marriage on the floor, and left.

Later that night, Ivy took Joseph by the hand and led him up the steps to her bedroom, much like she imagined Liam had done with Scarlett many times. She let him see her. She let him touch her. She let him have her in ways only her husband had for so very long. She didn't think of how Liam's hand felt on her hips as she moved on top of him. She didn't think of Liam's full lips tugging at her breasts, and she didn't recall how he told her he loved her so damn much when they were nearly finished.

"And you just stood there? You didn't say anything?" Tia's voice was loud over the cell phone that Ivy whispered into as she sat on the couch.

"It wasn't worth it. I had nothing to say to her or him."

"You let her take your husband and be around your babies when he didn't ask for your permission; why are you letting him take advantage of your personal time and allowing that whore to disrespect you on the street in front of your kids and Joseph?"

Ivy was speechless. Usually, Tia is Ivy's voice of reason, but tonight, she was irrational and unreasonable in the darkness.

"I'm sorry. I didn't mean to get so upset. I think that I'm stressed about my mom. Regardless, you deserve better, Ivy."

"I do deserve better." Ivy cleared her throat. "I slept with Joseph tonight."

"You're lying?!"

Ivy giggled. She was happy and felt alive for the first time in a long time.

"I promise." She whispered so the man sleeping upstairs in her bed didn't hear her.

"And? Well, how was it? How do you feel?" Tia waited anxiously for her best friend to answer.

"Happy. I'm happy."

She could hear Tia smile through the phone somehow.

"Listen, I'm sorry your mom is so sick. Is there anything I can do?"

Tia sighed, "I just want the breathing to stop. She just lays there, very still. And when she breathes, you can't see that she's breathing, but you can hear it. It's like this deep, raspy, gurgling sound. When she does it, I sit by her bed and count. It feels like I count to a thousand, but it's only almost a minute. Almost exactly fifty-three seconds every time. One time I counted to fifty-seven seconds, and just when I thought it was finally over, she took a breath."

"Tia, that sounds awful. I think you need a break. Do you want me to come be with you? I can be there by noon if I leave now."

"No. It's almost over. I'll be fine. It's just the waiting. Tonight, before I returned to her house, I stayed until midnight by her bedside and whispered close to her ear, *I hate you. I hate you for everything you did, but mostly for everything you didn't.* The woman has made my life so chaotic; even in death, she completely consumes me. And it's true; I do hate her. The only relief is that once this cancer eats her up and she is gone, I don't get rejected anymore. It's over for her, and it's over for me." Ivy knew tears were falling freely down her friend's face. She could hear her pain through the phone and let her cry and talk as long as she needed.

It wasn't until Ivy's eyes popped open around 4 am that she realized she had fallen asleep downstairs on the couch. Something had awakened her, and she was too exhausted and confused to care as she searched in the darkness for her phone. Then, she heard the noise that had startled her. Someone was in the house. She heard footsteps going down the hall. Ivy wanted to call out for Joseph; maybe he was trying to leave and not wake her. But he would have left out the front door. Perhaps he had forgotten something and was going back for it. She froze; she tried not even to breathe, so she could hear what the person was doing, rummaging through things in the kitchen. After a few seconds, the steps were coming toward her. She lowered back down onto the couch beneath the chenille throw. She pretended to be asleep. As exhausted and confused as she was before, she was wide awake now. Her heart beat so hard in her chest she could barely breathe. The steps were coming closer. And closer. Now Ivy could feel someone standing over her. They were watching her. She could hear them breathing. They didn't breathe anything like what Tia described over the phone earlier. They breathed in slowly and exhaled silently. Ivy didn't move. She willed her heart to go ahead and stop before she felt any pain from the intruder. What did they want? To rape her? Rob her? Kill her? Either way, she was thankful the kids weren't home; they were at Liam's. *Liam,* she thought. She wished Liam was here. She wished he was home, protecting her and his family like he used to do.

A light turned on at the top of the stairs. "Ivy?"

Fear spread over Ivy's body like chills on a cold wintery day. The person didn't panic and then run out the door as expected. The tall, dark shadow came closer to her and smelled her hair. Ivy nearly cried out. But then the figure stood, turned, walked slowly toward the front door, and left. It was as if no one was ever there. As if she dreamed it. Only she didn't.

Chapter Thirty-Two

NOW

Time was running out. I watched the second hand on my watch tick, tick tick away as I thought long and hard about it. I had a plan. Get in. Get out. I want to know everything about her. What décor does she hang on the walls? Does she keep her kitchen nice and tidy, or are there sippy cups and leftover plates strewed over the countertops and in the sink? What does she wear when she sleeps? What does she smell like? There's something special about her, something that makes her better. And I have to know what it is. I can only look at the hints of her life on social media so much. I know what she wants the world to know. But I want to know what no one else does.

I merely blinked, and I was standing on her front porch. The darkness shielded me from the rest of the world. I was prepared to break in, but as luck would have it, it wasn't locked when I quietly turned the doorknob. One gentle push, and I was in. Closing the door behind me, I could do what I wanted. It was as if I was on the playground at the park and had the whole place to myself. It wasn't swings, slides, and merry-go-rounds I was interested in. It's her. Delighted, and much to my surprise, I found her sleeping alone on the couch. This was too easy. I pulled one glove off with my teeth and kneeled beside her. Her skin was warm and soft. Her hair smelled of shampoo and the beach. I wondered what would happen if I moved my hand down to her throat, and then I climbed on top of her while I closed off her airway with my two bare hands. Well, one hand was bare now, the other still protected by a black leather glove. I'd let her squirm, let her feel fear, immense fear. So much fear that fear itself might be the thing that kills her, not by affixation.

She must have felt my presence because she began to stir. I didn't scurry, didn't hide. The darkness protected me. I watched her reposition herself on the soft sofa and then slide back into a deep sleep. Hate stirred. Fire boiled the blood in my veins. She is special. She's nearly a perfect creature. In fear of possibly doing just as I imagined moments before, I stood so I didn't strangle the life out of her. As I turned to make my way through the house and down the hall, my foot nearly kicked something across the room. I stopped and listened for her. What would I do if she woke up? I heard nothing, so I moved on, more carefully this time. I needed to get what I came for and go. Tonight isn't the night. I have to take things she cares about before I take her.

The kitchen was just as I suspected. Clean as a whistle. I could eat off the floor. I ran my hand over the cold countertop then, just as I had hoped, I saw what I came for. Two seconds later, I was coming back down the hallway, focusing on the front door. I had tucked what I wanted so badly into my pocket. It was time to go. But, the urge was too strong. I needed one more smell. Then I left. And I know she watched me as I closed the door and smiled.

Chapter Thirty-Three

NOW

"I guess I just forgot to lock the door last night. It was awful, Liam. I thought I was going to die."

Liam's chest was quickly rising and falling as his mind raced. He was scared, angry, and felt helpless all at the same time.

"Then what did you do?"

"Joseph came downstairs; I was scared and upset, so he held me for a few minutes; then we looked around, but nothing was missing. He tried to get me to call the police, but what was I supposed to say?"

Ivy waited for Liam to say something over the phone. She was panicking all over again, telling him what had happened. "Liam, are you there?"

She heard him let out a breath. "I'm here. I'm listening. I'm just…I mean, what the hell? I'll call and have a home security system put in immediately, and we should let the police know. They may find something you didn't. Damn, this is just mind-blowing."

There was only silence until Liam heard a muffled cry. "Are you okay? I'm so sorry this happened, Ivy. I'm glad you weren't hurt."

"I'm going to be okay. It was just so terrifying. I tried so hard to be still."

Silence, again.

"Can I ask you something, Ivy?"

"Of course." She answered, curious.

"Did you sleep with him? Last night? For the first time?" Liam held his breath as he waited for her to answer. He was crouched on the front steps of his rental house. The heat was causing beads of sweat to collect on his face.

She hesitated, daring to omit the truth and dance around with lies, but answered truthfully anyway, "Yes," she whispered.

Liam squeezed his eyes shut as hard as he could, but the tears still fell. He felt like he might get sick. He held the phone to his ear with one hand, and the other was pressed over his face. It was the only comfort he could find. A sob escaped him. And his chest jerked.

He had no right to ask, and he had no right to be so upset. But he was. He couldn't help it. He stood and wandered around the front yard. He didn't know if he should sit in the dirt, throw the phone, punch something or scream. Ultimately, he did none of those things. He swallowed hard and kneeled on the ground, trying to calm the storm raging inside of him. He saw flashes of Joseph's hands on his wife's skin. Flashes of the two of them doing everything he and Scarlett had done on the lake just yesterday.

"I'm sorry, Liam. I just… it's time. You know, to move on. I care about Joseph. A lot. He's been here for me through everything. And he cares about the kids. He cares about me." Her voice was low but no longer a whisper.

"You have nothing to apologize for, Ivy. Don't be sorry. It's none of my business. I just…" he took a deep breath and regained his composure, "I didn't expect to feel this way. This is just so hard. I hate this. I miss you, but I'm in love with…." He stopped.

He could feel the strike of his tongue hit her hard all the way across town. Then the silence over the phone was long. "I'm sorry." He whispered.

"You don't have to explain yourself to me, Liam. I'm your ex-wife now. We are simply co-parenting, nothing more. And that's all we will ever be. I've got to go."

"Wait, let me…" She hung up before he could finish. But he continued anyway. "Let me tell you one thing. You are the love of my life. The mother of my children. The one person I will always love most in this world besides our kids. And whether it's him or someone else, today, tomorrow, or fifty years from now… I'm always going to hurt when you are with someone else. The other day, in the doorway, I wanted to choose you. I wanted to kiss you back. I wanted to come inside and stay with you and the kids forever. But you will never forget what I did. And you will never forgive me. And I can't drive you mad again. I won't do that to you. You can't worry all the time. You can't remember all the time. So, I had to go." Liam stopped talking, then let the phone fall to the ground. He rubbed his rough hands over his wet face. "And I am in love with Scarlett. I'm so sorry, Ivy. I wish I weren't. But I am."

This Sunday was a monster. And Liam let it take him.

Chapter Thirty-Four

NOW

The night arrived on time; darkness encircled Ivy's house little by little as she watched the sun inch lower and lower into the abyss, then she whispered *goodbye.* Fear wrapped around her like a python, squeezing her to death.

The kids are tucked into their beds, all the doors are locked, and Ivy's phone is fully charged. She checked her phone twice before removing the charger connected to the wall outlet behind her nightstand in her quiet bedroom. Now it's gripped tightly in her sweaty right hand. Most of the lights in the house are on, and the blinds are closed. It's not late, but it feels like it should be. Time moves slowly when you are anxious for the morning sunlight to reveal everything the darkness is hiding.

A text comes across her phone. It's Joseph telling her he wants to stay the night with her. He even offers to sleep on the couch. Ivy considers but kindly declines his offer. She needs to be alone. She hasn't had time to process what happened between them in her bed last night. She had only thought of the person who came into her home uninvited while she slept.

Nothing feels the same. Everything is different now. Because of both Joseph and the intruder. And because of Liam. Why did he have to cry? It made her feel guilty for sharing more of herself with another man. And she shouldn't feel that way. The clock on the wall upstairs ticked and tocked. She listened to every little thing. She refused to let her guard down. If someone came close to her house, she would know it. This time she wouldn't freeze. She would fight.

Her fingers slid over the sharp blade. Not too close, though. The steel was cold. Ivy pulled the blanket close as she lay in the same place on the couch as the night before.

She hadn't told Tia what had happened. She couldn't. Tia lost her mom this morning. She didn't *lose* her; her mother left this earth. Ivy imagined the ailing mother had probably only left one hell for another. She hoped that once silence replaced the dying gurgling sounds and the coffin was lowered six feet into the ground and covered with dirt; Tia would have peace. But Ivy doubted that she would. Even after the people we love hurt us and then leave, we still feel their absence sleeping beside us. They never really go. You hear them breathing when they aren't. You smell them. You grow to hate them more. Because you loved them more than they loved you. They go, and you stay, inheriting all the memories and pain.

Ivy's heavy eyes closed as she rested her head on the throw pillow. The lamp across the room allowed some light to shine dimly across the ceiling.

Suddenly, Ivy's eyes opened. She didn't know why. Maybe it was because she realized she had fallen asleep or needed a drink of water. Her mouth was as dry as a sandy desert. Then she realized why she was awake. She could feel the person on the other side of her front door. A shimmer of the steel blade caught her eye. It had fallen onto the floor. She picked it up and listened carefully. Her eyes focused so hard on the door she didn't notice the tears that slowly trickled from her eyes and down her face. Then she watched as the knob turned right, then left. Slowly. Ivy stood. She wouldn't let them in this time. She had kids to protect tonight. But, no matter how hard the shadow outside tried to get in, they couldn't. Just as Ivy dashed for her phone on the coffee table to call the police, the knob stopped turning. Everything went silent except for Ivy's heart. She ran to the door to ensure she had locked it earlier, and it was. She waited and listened. She moved closer to the door and pressed her ear to the wood. She began to count. One, two, three.... all the way to fifty-three. And then there was breathing. Ivy swore she could hear breathing. She pressed her ear even harder against the wood, her hand shaking. But then she realized the person hadn't left. And they weren't breathing. They were laughing.

Chapter Thirty-Five

NOW

It was risky. And it was stupid. I don't know why I went back. I knew she would be waiting for me to return. She would be on the other side of the door she had locked long before the darkness of night arrived, and she would be prepared. And I was right.

I wanted her to be scared. I wanted her to know I would return, night after night. And I wanted her to know that I would never forgive her. She hurt me. And now, I would hurt her like a creepy crawly in the night. Next time, she won't suspect anything when I come for her. But I'm not taking anything from her purse next time. Next time I'll take the things she loves most.

Chapter Thirty-Six

NOW

Since Liam's phone alerted him that he had a text message at 4:53 pm this morning, he felt strange. Something wasn't right. He could feel it in his bones. After he read that the person had come back to Ivy's house that night, he called her. Her voice was so shaken he barely recognized it was her at all. He promised her that he would be right there. It wasn't until he ended the call that he realized Scar was standing in the bathroom doorway. Her head cocked to one side, her long arms crossed over her chest.

"Let me guess. Your ex-damsel is in distress, and you are off like a knight in shining armor to save the day?"

"That's not fair, Scar. The kids are there. What if he comes back?" Liam stood, pulled his boxers from the floor, and then looked for his jeans. He needed to hurry, but he could barely see in the dark as he rummaged through their small bedroom, searching for anything at this point to wear.

"I'll go with you." Scarlett walked over to the chest of drawers, but Liam stopped her before she could even open a drawer.

"No, Scar," he hugged her from behind, "I'll check everything out and be right back. If she sees you, she will just get upset, and things will be worse."

"Fine. Go." Scarlett crawled back into bed and pulled the covers up to her chin.

Moments later, she felt Liam kiss her cheek. "I love you. I'll be right back. I promise." And then he kissed her again.

But somehow, 5 am turned into noon. "I have sandwiches and ice-cold lemonade." Ivy sat a tray full of goodies onto the picnic blanket Liam and the kids sat on in the yard as they watched the two men work tirelessly to install the new security system.

Liam wiped Kimber's hands, which had gotten dirty from playing outside all morning. Then he helped her take a bite of a ham and cheese sandwich. Liam couldn't help but smile when she scrunched her nose after tasting the sour lemonade.

"Oh, shoot. I'll be right back. I forgot the fruit tray."

Before Ivy could get up, Liam stopped her. "You sit. I'll go grab it."

"Thank you, Liam." Ivy took over, encouraging their rambunctious almost two-year-old to eat her lunch.

Once inside, Liam tried to call Scar. She hadn't replied to any of his texts. His call was sent to voicemail. He sighed and rubbed his eyes as he walked down his old hallway toward the kitchen. Holden was barking outside, and Ben was laughing. Liam sat on the stool at the kitchen bar. He needed a minute. He laid his face in his hands and closed his tired eyes. If Liam kept his eyes closed and listened, it sounded like he was home.

His phone buzzed; it was a work email. Not Scar. Disappointment swirled inside him. When he went back outside, he would ask the guy how much longer this installation would take, and the minute they finished, he would leave and go to Scar at the office. He'd hold her and tell her he was sorry. She'd forgive him. She always did.

Chapter Thirty-Seven

NOW

The steak on the grill sizzled, and Liam's stomach growled. It was nearly time for Scar to get home from work. Considering she used her lunch hour to drive by his ex-wife's house to check up on him and skip out on eating actual lunch, Liam assumed she would be hungry. He was nervous to see her. He realized he wasn't good at balancing his old life and a new one simultaneously. The week they had the kids was so easy. But ever since the day he took them home and Ivy kissed him, everything seemed to come with a challenge.

Liam hoped he and Scar could enjoy a nice dinner outside, have drinks, listen to music, and then call it a night early. He needed to feel her in his arms. He missed her today. He will tell her that, but she won't believe him.

Right on time, the black four-door Audi with tinted windows pulled onto the gravel drive. Liam appreciated the shade from the tall tree standing in the yard, but now the sun was fading, and even in the darkness, Liam could see the disappointment on his girlfriend's beautiful face.

"Hey, babe." Liam closed the grill and walked to her as she followed the sidewalk into the house.

"Not right now, Liam." Scarlett's heels tapped over the concrete. "I need a shower."

Liam let her pass him, and he waited on her. It was nearly an hour after Liam set the patio table before she returned. The food was cold and the drinks were warm. Liam was exhausted.

Scarlett sat, then took a sip of her wine.

Liam didn't speak. He pulled his plate close and then began slicing the cold meat. It was silent for only a few minutes but felt like hours.

"I saw you today." Scarlett's voice was low.

"I know. I saw you today too." Liam didn't look up. He swallowed a bite of his baked potato and then pushed the plate aside.

"You looked like one big happy family." Scarlett wiped a tear away and followed suit by pushing her plate aside as well. She had barely touched any of the food.

Nothing about this evening had gone as planned. Maybe Liam should have driven into the city to see her earlier instead of waiting for her to come home.

"That's not fair, Scar." Liam took a swig of warm beer from his long-neck bottle.

"You know what's not fair, Liam? This. All of it. You divorced her. You left her. You asked me to live with you. You share your children with me, yet I'm still the mistress."

"That's ridiculous." Liam's expression changed, and he felt anger rise to his throat, making the alcohol taste sour. "I do everything I possibly can to make you not feel that way, Scarlett."

"Everything, really? If she and I were on fire at the same time on opposite sides of a burning house, who would you run to, Liam? Who would you save?"

Liam didn't answer. He only listened to the intensity in her voice grow.

"But you know what, Liam? I'm not the person on fire in this relationship. I've never been the one running out of a burning house needing to be saved. You are. And that's all I have been doing this whole time. Saving you from your failing marriage. Saving you from your heartbreaking divorce after, if I might add, you abandoned me, only to crawl back when she couldn't get over the fact that you had sex with me. Then I had to save you when you were alone, and she wouldn't let you come home." Her voice was starting to crack. Tears trickled down her cheeks. "There is nothing in this world I want more than you. Still. But you're burning me, Liam. You're hurting me. Every time you see her, every time she gets hurt, every time she gets scared... you go to her. And I'm here. The woman who only gets a piece of you. And she's still the woman who gets more, and she's not even your wife anymore, Liam."

"No, but she is the mother of my kids, Scarlett. I'm just doing my best to take care of my family and you at the same time." His words hung in the air, like the stale smell of the grease on the cold grill. He thinks the fat might taste better than the words he just spoke to her. Regret surged through his chest.

"I'm supposed to be your family too." She was crying now.

Scarlett stood and went into the house. Liam took a deep breath and, for the second time today, he placed his face in his hands, feeling defeated.

He planned to give Scarlett a little space and then go inside and apologize for what he said and how he treated her. She was right. He does still feel things when he sees Ivy. He breaks when Joseph is near her. He's still trying to let go entirely. It's just taking some time. He told Scarlett he wanted to go slow, but then everything started moving too fast. Faster than he could run.

The front screen door slammed, Liam's head jerked up, and he saw Scarlett with her overnight bag on her shoulder and carrying her purse in her other hand.

"You're leaving?" Liam sounds like he doesn't care, but he swears he does.

She ignored him as she threw the leather bag onto the backseat and opened the driver's side door.

"Where are you going, Scarlett?"

Scarlett searched her purse for the phone instead of answering him.

"Scarlett, talk to me!"

"I have nothing more to say. Goodbye, Liam." In a flash, the door shut, the engine roared, and she backed out of the gravel driveway and disappeared.

Liam barely entered the house when he received Ivy's text saying she couldn't set the new alarm system. He nearly threw the phone against the wall, cursing and trying not to scream. Just as he started out the front door, she texted back that she had figured it out.

Liam dialed Scarlett. He didn't mind if she answered and screamed at him. He just wanted her to answer. But she didn't. And just like that, he was on fire. And she wasn't there to put it out this time.

Chapter Thirty-Eight

NOW

"Sorry about that. The babysitter thinks the new alarm system at the house is offline, and she couldn't figure out how to set it. But she got it. Finally." Ivy dropped her phone back into her oversized bag sitting beside her on the floor of her favorite little restaurant.

"No worries, I'm just happy you installed one, and hopefully, whoever has been coming to your house at night will stop or get caught."

"Me too." Ivy agreed with Tia and took a sip of the cold water. The humidity was thick tonight as they sat on the patio sharing an entrée. "How are you doing? I mean, with your mom and everything?" Ivy knew this was a sensitive subject, but Tia looked tired. She had been spending late nights on the hospital's Hospice Floor, driving many hours back and forth for work, and now dealing with the estate. She looked worse than tired. She looked exhausted.

"I wish I could say it happened quickly, but it didn't. It was slow. I wasn't sad. I don't know what I was, but it wasn't sad." Tia laid the black cloth napkin over her plate.

"You just need some time to process it, Tia. Her life was complicated, and so was her death. Grief will come later; you have to forgive and heal first."

"I'm so glad you think you know exactly how I feel all the time." Tia scoffed and took a sip of her water. Condensation dripped down the side of the thick glass.

"What do you mean?" Ivy nearly fell to the floor. Tia had never spoken to her like this before.

"You don't know everything about everything all the time, Ivy. There are things you don't know that would blow your little mind. Things like…" Tia stopped.

The air was thick, but the confusion caught in Ivy's throat, nearly choking her, was thicker. Even if she knew the right words to say, she couldn't speak them.

"I'm sorry. That wasn't nice. I need to go."

Ivy watched in shock as her friend gathered her things and threw money onto the table.

"Please, don't go. Let's talk about this." Ivy pleads with her.

But Tia rose to her feet anyway.

"I just need to tell you…."

Tia interrupted her, "That's just it, Ivy. You are always needing to tell me something. I am sick of hearing what you constantly need to tell me. I don't want to hear about Liam. Or Scarlett. It's over! Move on, Ivy!"

Ivy watched Tia storm away down the sidewalk, disappearing into the darkness. Ivy was confused and hurt. But she knew that Tia was right. It is over, and she does need to move on.

Ivy looked at the people sitting around them, all staring back at her. Her cheeks grew red with embarrassment.

Tomorrow is her and Liam's wedding anniversary. Well, it's not much of an anniversary anymore. Ivy made a promise to herself as she sat alone at the table, listening to everyone around her laughing and talking beneath the strings of lights hanging over them, and it reminded her of the night she met Liam. Silently, she promised herself she could have tomorrow. She could feel it. Every minute of it. She'd remember that special day, along with all the promises. She would allow herself to be sad and cry. But after tomorrow, it's over. No matter what happens, she won't call Liam. Unless it's about the kids, the line of communication is nothing. Her happiness, conversations, and life will no longer be centered around her marriage and divorce. After tomorrow. She promises.

Moments later, as Ivy drove home, she noticed that the car following her took every turn that she did while keeping a safe distance. So she passed her house. Then she passed the next subdivision. She reached for her phone to call Liam but stopped when the car finally turned. Ivy noticed the number she had pulled up on the phone in her hand. She had almost pressed the screen to call him, but she hadn't. She dropped the phone onto the passenger seat and took a deep breath. This promise was going to be harder to keep than she thought.

Chapter Thirty-Nine

NOW

Some moments can change us forever. In one second, you can win or lose everything. Sometimes those things are one of the same. But after that moment, your whole world is altered. And you just know nothing will ever be the same again. Grief is immediate. Panic surges through your guts, and you can't speak. You just move through the motions of life. You don't know whether to cry, scream, or fall to your knees and surrender. But you do none of those things. You just go. You do everything you would normally do in a tragic situation, and you are hyper-aware of everything happening around you but utterly oblivious at the same time. At least, that is how Liam feels right now in this very moment. The blue lights on top of the police cars are flashing, but the alarms are silent. He can hear sirens in the distance, though; more police are coming. The officers wear covers over their shoes as they search for evidence around the playground area and near the river bank. Their shoe covers are muddy. The swing farthest away from where he and Ivy are sitting is swinging with the breeze as if a small child were sitting in it. He prayed it wasn't one of his children's ghosts. He imagined Ben holding on to the silver chains as he kicked his feet in the air, making the swing go higher and higher.

Police car scanners and the officer's radios on their hips were noisy. Cars were trying to enter the small park, but the police were directing them to leave. No one was to enter.

"Please! I'm begging you; I'm okay; please go find my kids!" Tears were pouring down Ivy's face, but she wasn't sobbing. The EMT held an ice pack to the side of her head. The blood in her hair had already dried. That meant that time had passed—too much time.

"She's right. What are we going to do? How do we find out what happened? Why are we just sitting here, damn it?!"

"Mr. Cameron, please stay calm. We have people searching the area, units patrolling the streets, and we are pulling all the camera footage possible. We will find your kids. The man with sagging skin hanging from his neck and bags under his eyes touched Liam's shoulder. A man who looks like that doesn't get a lot of sleep, probably because he's seen a lot of things. Bad things.

Liam thought the man was trembling but quickly realized it was Ivy sitting next to him who was shaking. Her whole body looked as if the weather were below zero outside. "Ivy, come here." He pulled her close; she laid her head on his shoulder and covered her face with her hands. The EMT worked around them, taking her blood pressure, then asking to look at her pupils.

The man talking over his radio had told him his name moments earlier, but Liam was watching those flashing lights on top of the car parked by the garbage can and didn't pay attention. Everything felt surreal, from the chaos on the ground to the birds flying high in the sky.

"Excuse me, I'm sorry, I forgot your name. But what can we do to help? I can't just sit here." Liam felt like the iciness had passed from Ivy to himself. He was shivering amidst the heat. He was cold, down to his bones.

"I'm Detective Karnes. A search party is assembling now. The best people I have on our rescue teams and many trusted people in the community will search the town and the river. While they do that, I will take you to your residence and set up a home base there, okay? And once I've asked you and Mrs. Cameron some questions, we will move on to the next best step, alright?"

Liam didn't want to leave. He needed to be with everyone else, calling out to Ben and Kimber. He needed to be in the truck searching every person, house, and car he passed. He had watched enough television to know that the parents are always suspects and time is of the essence.

"Okay. Whatever we need to do." Liam pulled Ivy closer.

"Mam, I'll load you into the ambulance, and we'll transport you to the hospital. We need to rule out a concussion, and you need a few stitches."

"Please, I'm begging you. Just stitch me up here. I can't be at the hospital right now. I need to help find my kids."

The twenty-something first responder started to respond but hesitated. "Come with me. Can you walk?" He held out a gloved hand to help her up.

"Yes, I'm fine." Ivy stood. Liam didn't realize he was holding her hand; he didn't want to let go. But he did then the EMT led her toward the ambulance with flashing emergency lights and no sirens.

"I'll be right back." She barely looked at Liam as she walked away, wincing in pain and holding her head.

Liam was alone. Hundreds of people were nearby, but he sat alone on the same old wooden bench where he proposed to Ivy and where they found out their second child was a girl. And now, this bench will always represent something very different. This memory will trump the others. Always.

Liam pulled his phone from his pocket and dialed Scarlett. His call went straight to voicemail. Liam pushed *end* and closed his eyes. All he could see was Ben and Kimber and their last moments together. Liam checked his phone to see if he had missed any texts from Scar, but he hadn't. Then he noticed the date. He had almost forgotten. It was his and Ivy's wedding anniversary. If they were still married, he would have been here with them today, and no one would have been able to hurt Ivy and take his kids. He should have been here. Tears stung his eyes, and rage filled his chest. Sometimes he's his own worst enemy, and he knows it.

He stood; he didn't know why; he just needed to stand. He turned in a circle, his eyes darting from the river to the forest, to the playground, to the cars in the parking lot. Where are his kids? Of course, whoever took them, is gone and not here. Liam's knees were growing weak.

He heard Ivy cry out in pain as the needle and thread pierced her skin in the back of the ambulance. He went to her and put her hand in his. She was still shaking. Her face was swelling.

"Looks like you've still got some old bruising and scarring from a recent injury."The EMT spoke as he worked.

"I was hiking with a friend and fell. I nearly went over a cliff." Ivy looked tired and weak. Much how Liam assumed he looked last night.

"One last stitch, and that should have it."

Ivy squeezed Liam's hand, reminding him of when she was in labor. She's braver than he is. She always has been. He brought her hand to his lips and kissed her skin while lightly stroking her long black hair. It's as soft and silky as it was that day they welcomed Kimber into the world.

Suddenly, Liam realized what he was doing, and he stopped. He stopped touching her hair and rested her hand on her thigh as she lay back on the gurney. It was just a natural thing to take care of her, to help her. He was sure those feelings were never going to go away. With or without Scar in his life. Or any woman, for that matter.

"All finished. Just keep the area clean. Follow up with your physician ASAP. Sooner with any signs or symptoms of infection or if you have any concerns of a possible concussion. And I'm keeping you guys in my prayers. I hope they find your kids very soon."

"Thanks, man." Liam shook the EMT's gloved hand, then helped Ivy off the gurney and out the back of the ambulance.

"Okay, you two, let's get to your house. It looks like they got you all patched up." Detective Karnes placed his phone inside his navy blue suit jacket, and they followed him to the parking lot.

Ivy felt her pockets for her keys, then panicked when she saw her purse still sitting on the bench where they were sitting when someone attacked her.

"One second." Ivy walked slowly back to the bench, then back to the parking lot.

"Actually, Mrs. Cameron, we have your car keys. We need the car to remain here for a while; then, we will return your vehicle once forensics is finished. It won't be long."

Ivy looked confused and started to protest, but Liam spoke up. "It's okay, Ivy. Let them do whatever they need to do. You can ride with me." He walked over to his truck and helped her inside.

Her legs were wobbly; he helped steady her.

"Straight to your residence. I'll be following behind you."The detective ordered Liam. Liam just nodded. He was still scoping out the people and cars around them.

"What if we never find them, Liam? What if they are gone forever?" Ivy started to cry.

And so did he. He didn't have words. He just did what he could. He pulled Ivy's hand to his lips and kept it there as she moved in close and rested her head on his shoulder all the way home.

Chapter Forty

NOW

Earlier today, Ivy had driven these same roads to the park. Ben and Kimber were buckled safe and sound in their car seats in the back. Ivy thought of Kimber's pink sippy cup with butterflies lying on the ground near the slide back at the park. She saw it while running around in circles screaming Kimber's name. She thought of the small yellow Tonka truck on the dirt pile. It was as if it was just abandoned there. Ben would never leave behind his toy. He takes care of his things.

The picnic basket full of lunch is still in her car, ruined by now. She had so carefully prepared a peanut butter and grape jelly sandwich for Kimber and a turkey and cheese sandwich for Ben and herself. She also included a few cut-up veggies and fruit—green seedless grapes for Kimber and blueberries for Ben, their favorites. One would also find something else inside that basket that wouldn't ordinarily be packed for a picnic with their kids; one long-stem, pale pink rose. Ivy decided that every year on their wedding anniversary, she would buy a dozen pale pink roses for herself. This morning she put them in the heavy crystal vase Liam had bought for her, the only one she hadn't thrown out, then placed them on the dining room table. She'd never tell anyone why; it was just something special for her, like someone placing flowers on a gravestone. Her marriage hadn't lasted, but it was like a fairytale for a while. Her fairytale. The days were written right out of a dream, and the nights were even more magical. Most of the time, anyway. So, she would always celebrate her wedding anniversary. She would celebrate one of the best things she ever did. She was madly in love with Liam and his children. Those things weren't nothing. Those things deserved to be celebrated long after the magic wand had been burned and the storybook grew dusty on a shelf no one reads from anymore.

Did she tell her kids that she loved them enough? Did she hug them enough? She wondered as Liam held her hand in his as she rested her throbbing head on his shoulder.

It shouldn't have been such a surprise to see the street she lived on was already packed with people, police, and even a news van. But she was. Somehow she imagined this much differently. Liam let go of her hand and sat straight as the bystanders cleared the middle of the street for them to get by. A police car led with its lights on and occasionally sounded the siren when people refused to move. It felt like a movie. This can't be happening for real.

The police car drove past the house, and Liam pulled his truck into the driveway. The detective pulled in directly behind him, very closely. Liam looked at Ivy, and they were sure they were thinking the same thing simultaneously. They were suspects in their own children's kidnapping. The parents always are until they are thoroughly questioned and cleared.

The detective tapped on Liam's window as people surrounded his truck, then instructed him to go straight to the house's front entrance, and he suggested they didn't make any comments to the media yet. The detective, who had witnessed too many horrors in his lifetime, informed him that there would be a press conference shortly, and they would speak to the public then.

Once Liam exited the truck, he came around and opened Ivy's door, and helped her lower herself onto the concrete. She then looped her arm around his, and they made their way through the chaos and into the house.

Immediately Ivy started to cry. Everywhere she looked, she saw pieces of Ben and Kimber. Kimber's little purple rainboots sat on the rug next to the door. Ben's bicycle helmet rested on the coffee table. All their things were here, but they felt so far away.

"Liam, Ivy. I'll give you a few minutes, and then Detective Roberts and I will sit down and review a few things.

"Sure, of course," Liam replied, then told Ivy he needed to use the restroom down the hall. She said she'd use the one in her bedroom to freshen up.

"Ivy. I'm sorry, but I'll need to send an officer with you, and please don't wash your hands or change clothes or anything. You can relieve yourself. But then we will need to scrape your nails and take your clothing.

"I can't believe you are treating her this way. She was attacked, and our children were taken, and you are practically accusing her of lying!" Liam's face turned red.

"Shhh, Liam, it's okay. It will be just fine. Let's do what they say and get it over with so they will start looking for the people who took Ben and Kimber."

She then turned to Detective Karnes, "Just do what you need to do. I don't need a minute."

Ivy sat on the couch across from the two detectives. Liam joined but didn't sit close to Ivy. This shouldn't bother her, but it did.

Detective Karnes sat an old-fashioned black recorder on the coffee table beside Ben's helmet. They all paused as a woman with gloves approached Ivy and began using a wooden tool to scrape beneath her nails, cut them, and then placed them in a clear bag with a blank label. After she and the woman went to the bathroom for Ivy to change her clothing, the woman took each article and placed them in separate clear bags with labels as well.

Once they returned, the woman gathered the bags and left. The detective turned on the recorder and stated the date, time, and who was present.

"Ivy, let's talk about the last twenty-four hours. Start by telling us your whereabouts and the children."

"Well, I was home with Liam and the kids while our home security system was installed. We were outside mostly. Then Liam left, our babysitter came, I met my friend for dinner, came home, the sitter left, and I went to bed." Ivy was calm and tried to recall everything the best she could.

"Who is your friend that you had dinner with?" The detective didn't look up at her; he stared down at his notepad and pen, ready for her answer so he could write it down.

"Her name is Tia Gaines."

"What restaurant and what time did you leave there?" Once again, he didn't look up, yet Detective Roberts didn't stop staring straight at her.

"We ended up calling it a night a little early, so around 7ish. I think."

"And why did you end the night early?"

"Hmm?" Ivy didn't know why that was relevant.

"You said you ended the night a little early, and I'm asking you why you departed dinner early. Did something happen between you and your friend?" This time he did look up and straight into her eyes.

"We had a little spat, so she left. I paid and left not long after."

"And you drove straight home, no stops?"

"I drove straight home."

"Did you leave your house any after that until this morning?"

"No. I did not. What does any of this have to do with what happened today?" Now Ivy's face was turning red.

"Please just answer the questions. This morning, what did you do?"

"I made the kids eggs and toast, we got dressed, I made our lunches for the park, and then we left."

"It looks like there was a floral delivery to your home this morning?"

"Yeah, so." Ivy looked at Liam nervously. She watched his jaw clench. She knew that he assumed the flowers were sent from Joseph. But they weren't; she would have to share her little secret and didn't want to.

"Do you know the sender? Did you recognize the delivery person? Just want to ensure that this isn't connected with what happened today."

Ivy hesitated and then cleared her throat as she rubbed her hands together in her lap. She hates this.

"I sent them to the house. For myself. Um, a dozen pale pink roses."

"Do you do this often? Send flowers to yourself, I mean?"

She hates him. "No. I don't. Today is my wedding anniversary, and pink roses are the first flowers Liam gave me and the flower we used in our wedding. It's just something I did for me."

"Are you referring to your marriage to Mr. Cameron?"

"Yes." She whispered.

"Please speak up, so the recorder can understand you."

"Yes, I am referring to my marriage to Liam. And there was nothing suspicious about the delivery person; they delivered on time."

"I see. And then, once you arrived at the park, tell me about the events leading up to the attack."

Ivy's heart started pounding so loudly she was sure the detective would hear it clearly on his stupid recorder."

"I just remember the kids playing. Kimber was near the slides, and Ben played with his truck in the dirt. Everything else is gone. Just black"

"You don't recall being hit on the head or seeing anyone already there when you arrived? Perhaps you noticed another car in the parking lot?"

"Like I said. I can't remember being attacked. No one was there when we were there. We were the only ones, the only car."

"Tell me about when you awoke."

"At first, I thought I was still in bed and was having a nightmare because all I knew was that my eyes were closed and my head was hurting. Very badly. Then I realized I was on the ground and the wind was blowing. I was confused and thought perhaps I was there alone, and then I saw Kimber's sippy cup and Ben's truck and remembered they had been there with me." Ivy swiped a tear that rolled down her cheek. Liam moved closer and held her hand. "I started searching for them and calling out their names. But no one answered, and I couldn't find them on the playground. I went to the river; they love to throw food to the fish. I panicked and thought maybe they had fallen in. But then I realized I was injured. Blood was all over my face, and my head hurt even more. That's when I knew someone knocked me out and took them." Ivy started crying too many tears to wipe away with her hands. Liam handed her a tissue from the box on the coffee table.

"Then what did you do?"

"I found my phone in my purse and called 9-1-1. Then I called Liam. The police came just after that."

Everything was quiet for a few minutes as the detectives compared notes and referred to other papers in their files.

"You're doing great," Liam whispered in her ear, and she moved into him as close as she could. Divorced or not, if she could crawl inside of him and hide forever, she would.

"Okay, Liam. Your turn. Whereabouts the last twenty-four hours. Go."

"As Ivy said earlier, I was here while the security system was installed. Then I left, went by the store, then home. Grilled steaks, ate with my girlfriend, then went to bed." Ivy noticed how the detective looked at Liam when he mentioned his girlfriend, yet he was holding on to Ivy for dear life.

"What's your girlfriend's name?"

Liam cleared his throat and sat up straight. As if guilt was punching him in the stomach for being this close to Ivy on the couch. "Scarlett Black." He replied loud and clear. The recorder definitely understood that response.

"And does Ms. Black live at the same residence as you?"

"Yes, she does."

"So, she was home with you all night?"

Liam hesitated and leaned forward, placing his elbows on his knees and clasping his hands in front of him. "No, not last night. We had a disagreement, and she left after dinner." Ivy searched his face to see if this made him sad, and she could tell it did. And that made her sad.

"Were you home all night until this morning, or did you leave at any time?"

"No, I was home until I left for work this morning."

"What were your whereabouts from the time you woke up until you arrived at the park?"

Liam swallowed hard. "I woke up, showered, had coffee, and drove into the city. I stopped by Scarlett's office before going to mine; we work on the same floor, I left for lunch, and that's when I got the call from Ivy and drove straight from the café down the street from where I work to the park."

"Was Ms. Black at her office when you stopped by this morning?"

"No, she wasn't. She's going through a lot right now, and I assume she took the day off."

"And did you go to lunch with anyone today?"

"No, I was alone."

Ivy touched Liam's hand, but he didn't respond. He resembled the man from the last few weeks instead of the Liam, who had been by her side earlier today.

Detective Roberts slid blank sheets of paper across the table and handed them pens. "Ivy, please write down contact info for your friend and the babysitter. Liam, I need your girlfriend's contact info, please."

They completed the information requested and slid the papers back to the detective, who was silent for most of the afternoon.

"I want to do a press conference in thirty minutes out on the lawn. I will speak on the facts of today's happenings, then introduce the two of you. You can ask the public to come forward with any information they might have and ask for volunteers to join the search party. We need as much help as possible, and sometimes, the perpetrator will return to the scene to be involved. We will evaluate every one. Do you have any questions?"

"No," Ivy answered.

Liam shook his head no.

"We will get everything set up outside. Let me know if you remember anything, Ivy. It would be helpful if you did."

"Of course," Ivy replied.

The detectives left through the front door. Liam and Ivy were all alone. No tiny voices were asking for cookies or a drink of apple juice. No cries nor laughter filled the house. It was just quiet.

Chapter Forty-One

NOW

"You've reached Scarlett Black. Leave a message, and I'll return your call. Thanks."

Liam loves to hear his girlfriend's voice but hates getting her voicemail. "Scar, it's me. Um, the kids are missing. Ivy was attacked at the park today, and someone took them." His voice started to crack, and he paused. "I just need you to call me. I love you." Liam pressed *end* and sat back on the couch, wishing Scarlett was there. He didn't care how awkward it would be. She was right last night. She is his family too. And she should be here, with him.

He called Scar again and was forwarded to her voicemail. It occurred to him that maybe they really are over.

"It's time." Detective Karnes ushered both Liam and Ivy outside to a podium. As soon as they exited the front door, Ivy's arm intertwined with his.

Liam noticed many familiar faces as the detective spoke into the small microphone. There were a lot of strangers as well, and he remembered what Detective Karnes said about the perpetrator wanting to be involved, and suddenly he was suspicious of everyone. Familiar or not. But one face wasn't there. And he wanted to know why. Where was Joseph while all this was going down? He could hear Holden barking in the backyard, and the clouds darkened the sky. He expected the world to stop today. It felt like his world had stopped. Everyone elses should as well. It wasn't fair.

The detective finished speaking and introduced them as Mr. Cameron and Ms. Cameron.

He listened as Ivy pleaded for help to find their children and relayed information about the search. Then she turned to Liam so he could step toward the microphone and speak to everyone standing on the lawn and watching from home. But he didn't have any more to say. Detective Karnes and Ivy had already said everything that needed to be said. But he stepped forward anyway.

"On behalf of Ivy and myself, we want to thank you for everything you're doing to assist in bringing our children back home to us. I encourage you to help in the search if you can, get their pictures out on social media, and if anyone knows anything, we ask that you come forward. Thank you." He stepped back beside Ivy, and she took his arm again. The detective concluded the press conference, and they returned inside the house without answering any questions.

Ivy went to the kitchen for a glass of water. The detectives instructed them to stay put, provided directions on how to answer their phones, and gave them his contact info if they needed him, then he was gone.

Liam sat on the second step of the stairway that led upstairs. He checked his phone. He was receiving a ton of texts from friends and family, but he didn't have words right now.

Ivy handed him a cold glass of ice water and sat beside him on the steps. They were alone again. It was quiet again.

The infamous clock on the wall upstairs ticked, but the seconds felt like hours. The sun was setting; the house was silent and growing dark. Ivy was trembling again. Liam pulled her close and let her cry. She pulled the throw up to her chin and sobbed into Liam's chest. Her arm laid over his thigh, her hand in his. His eyes scanned over her sleeve of tattoos. At one time, he had kissed every single one. He let go of her hand and traced the tattoos with his thumb. Every now and then, he felt scratches on her skin. She had chosen all his favorite colors, all their favorite places, and even a pale pink rose. A whole life imprinted into her skin forever. It was a good life. He couldn't help but feel responsible. Had he made better choices, today would have gone differently. He nearly choked on regret and had to swallow hard.

"Don't. Don't do that." Ivy whispered.

"What?"

"I know what you're thinking, and you're wrong. None of this is your fault."

"I'm sorry, Ivy. For everything." His whisper was so low she could barely hear him.

"I know you are. I'm sorry I drove you away. I'm sorry that I didn't get help. I'm sorry I forgave you when it was too late." She looked into his eyes.

Today, on the worst day of his life, her eyes were just as beautiful as when they met. That was the best night of his life. He wasn't sure if he should, but he touched his lips to hers, and she tasted like when she was his.

She rested her hand on the side of his face; for a second, today wasn't today. They were somewhere far away, married and celebrating their wedding anniversary.

He didn't know how he was already inside her; nothing happening was calculated or intentional. It was as if they were on autopilot mode, doing what they had always done to feel close to one another, to fix whatever was ailing them. It was a natural, loving act of love; married or not. Tears-streaked Ivy's face as she moved. When it was over, Liam held her tight and let her cry.

Then, the front door opened without warning, and Liam stared straight into Joseph's eyes. Even in the darkness, Liam could see his pain and confusion.

But Liam didn't move, didn't push Ivy away, or apologize. He just stayed. But Ivy jumped, covered herself, and ran to him.

"Joseph! Don't go. Please." Ivy tugged at Joseph's arm, but he pulled away. She looked stunned and hurt. She stepped back, allowing his pained eyes to stare into hers. "I'm sorry," she whispered.

Joseph stopped looking at Ivy and turned his attention to Liam, who was still sitting on the staircase. Joseph looked at him with disgust, shook his head, and scoffed as he left and slammed the door behind him.

Then, Liam stood, pulled his suit pants up, and fastened his belt. Ivy didn't speak to him; she gathered her clothes, went to her bedroom, and closed the door.

Liam knew all the right curse words, all the walls around him to punch, and all the prayers he needed to pray for forgiveness. But he was just too tired. He simply picked up the little doll on the living room rug, sat on the couch, and waited. He waited for someone to bring his kids back to him. He waited for Ivy to come back downstairs so he wouldn't be alone. He waited for Scarlett to call. He wondered if this would be his life from now on. Waiting. And alone.

Chapter Forty-Two

NOW

It was almost too easy. No one saw anything, nor did anyone know anything. It was done. I took the children. And soon, I'll have him too.

Chapter Forty-Three

NOW

"We had to call off the on-foot search until morning due to the weather conditions. We will set up camp here tonight." Detective Karnes had papers spread across the dining room table. Officers were coming and going from the house; all the lights felt brighter, causing Liam's eyes to burn, and the sounds were louder, making his head pound. Liam felt alone, even with Ivy next to him.

One of the officers said they had footage from the convenience store down the street from the park. A large laptop played, and they all watched, searching the screen, not blinking in fear they would miss something. And that's when Liam noticed the familiar vehicle. The one he watched drive down the street as he sat with Ivy and the kids on the picnic blanket the day before and the same vehicle he watched back out of his driveway last night. A black four-door Audi.

Even with the tinted windows, you could see her strawberry-blonde hair.

He nearly fainted. This had to be a mistake. Why? How?

"Was that Scarlett's car, Liam?" Ivy asked loudly.

He couldn't speak.

"Liam!" she screamed.

"Yes, I think so."

In that second, everything went crazy. The police were talking over scanners of an APB, descriptions of his girlfriend's vehicle were being relayed to one another, and someone mentioned an all-points bulletin.

Liam knew it was strange, but he felt some relief. He knew if Scar took the kids because of some breakdown or insanity, she would never harm them. She loved them.

"Liam, have you talked to her today?!" Ivy was in his face as he sat at the table, unable to move.

"No. She hasn't answered any of my calls."

"You better go find her right now; I swear if she hurts my kids, I will kill her." Ivy was furious. Her arms thrashed in the air; she looked like a mad woman.

"Why aren't you angry, Liam?!"

"Because if she did take them, she'd never hurt them, Ivy. It's better than some child predator or crazy person on the street."

"You are unbelievable. If you don't hate her for this, you don't deserve to be their father."

"I am their father, Ivy. No matter what. And I always will be." He stood, causing his chair to fall and crash against the hardwood floor.

"Not if she kills them. Then you will have no one."

Ivy left the room, and this time Liam found that wall to punch.

Chapter Forty-Four

NOW

Ivy was shaking again. Not because she was scared this time, but because she was so mad she couldn't stand it. "I'm so angry I don't know what to do. I let her take you, and now she has taken my kids. And what makes me absolutely furious is that you aren't angry with her!" She couldn't understand why Liam wasn't as mad as she was. It didn't make any sense.

"She didn't take me, Ivy. I made my own choices. And I am angry. I want answers too. None of this makes any sense." Liam ran his hand through his hair.

The sun started peering through the curtains, and the light shone across the bedroom floor. No one could find any more answers about where Scarlett had gone after passing by the convenience store yesterday. Her phone was off, and her car could not be located. It was as if she had disappeared into thin air.

"Do you think people can disappear? Just like that? Poof?"

Liam didn't answer. He just held her as they lay in bed on top of the covers. It was an unreasonable question.

They had drifted to sleep a couple of times, but one always woke the other. They had suspected that it was also Scarlett who had come to Ivy's house those two nights before the kidnapping. Liam didn't know if he was in denial or just knew in his gut that everyone was wrong. So he stayed quiet, continued letting the authorities do their job, and listened to their instructions. Besides the kids, his biggest worry was that he could tell Ivy was fading. She was succumbing to the stress and exhaustion. She reminded him of the Ivy that drove into the tall tree beside the road with the kids that rainy night he told her about his affair. She looked like a woman who was losing it. He couldn't save her then, and he can't save her now. But he was doing his best.

"I'd like some coffee. I'm going to make us some coffee." Ivy rolled over in bed to face him. Their eyes locked. Her eyes were different now. They were the eyes Ivy wore when she was struggling with reality and slipping. It scared him.

"I'll come with you," Liam whispered.

"No, stay here." She whispered back.

"I love you, Liam. I know you know that." A tear slowly slid down her cheek.

He couldn't say it back. A piece of him would always love her, but more of him loved the woman no one could find right now. And he'd have to hate her eventually. Right now, he was numb.

Ivy got out of bed, still dressed in the same clothes she had changed into after they made love on the steps last night.

This was a nightmare. A real nightmare.

Once she left the bedroom they used to share, she closed the door behind her, and Liam lay in silence, looking at the pictures of the kids in frames on the walls and dresser. All good moments. Great moments.

Ivy is still the same. Not a thing in the room is out of place. Every little nook and cranny is spotless. Liam used to drive her crazy; he would sometimes leave clothes on the floor or place his wallet on the dresser beside the wooden bowl and not in it. He did his best to live by her standards most of the time.

But one thing is out of place, though. One of his ball caps lay on the chest of drawers. One he hadn't seen in a while.

Liam desperately wanted a hot shower and some clean clothes. He wondered by chance if Ivy had kept anything of his he might be able to wear. The closet was bare except for Ivy's things. He pulled a couple of drawers open until he found one with only a T-shirt. That T-shirt didn't belong to him; it was Joseph's. Liam shut the drawer. He remembered having some old clothes boxed up in the attic, and sure enough, there were several totes and boxes with his name written on them along the wall to the right. The clothes would smell musty, but he was desperate.

He rummaged through one container, but it was all winter sweaters and dress clothes that would most definitely be too small. As he removed the lid to another container, he smelled the aroma of fresh hot coffee.

"Whatcha doing up here?" Ivy coughed a little from the dust stirring in the air and handed Liam his cup of coffee while trying not to spill her own.

"I'm just trying to find anything to change into. But I'm not having any such luck."

"I didn't even realize you had all this stuff up here." Ivy sat her coffee cup down and opened up an old cardboard box from Liam's apartment from when they first met.

It was full of old baseball cards, college notebooks, papers, and mail.

"I think I can still fit into my old grad school shirt and this pair of jeans." Liam held up some clothing to show her, but Ivy couldn't tear her eyes away from something she had found at the bottom of Liam's old box long ago. Long before she was in Liam's life.

"What is it?" Liam didn't replace the lid on the container; he left it on the dusty wood-planked floor.

"Who is this woman?" Ivy couldn't let go of the photo in her hands.

Liam walked behind her to see the photo and who she was talking about. It only took one glance for him to recognize the pretty girl leaning in to him. Both of his arms were wrapped around her. Both of them were smiling, laughing, really. He remembered that day well; it was high school graduation day.

"She was my high school girlfriend. I told you about her. Her name was Robin. Robin Gaines."

Ivy couldn't believe what she was seeing. There was no mistaking the long curly blonde hair, her green eyes, or that one little scar just above her upper lip. "I know her." She didn't mean for her words to come out as a whisper, but they did.

"What? How do you know my high school girlfriend?" Liam was confused.

Ivy swallowed hard, "She told me her name was Tia. Tia Gaines. She's my best friend."

Liam watched as all the color left Ivy's face. "Ivy, I don't understand. How did you meet her?"

"I met her at the BOOK NOOK. You know that old bookstore downtown I like to go to?" She noticed that Liam's eyes were probably as wide as hers.

"Yes, I know the one." Liam glanced back down at the picture; his face was sure to be as pale as Ivy's now.

"I was having a bad day, it was just after I filed for divorce, and she complimented the book I was looking at. I had been debating whether I was going to buy it or not. She was very friendly, and we talked about books for a long time." Ivy scratched at her cheek, trying to recall the rest of that day. "And then I had to go, and she suggested we exchange numbers because we read and enjoyed the same types of books. So, I gave her my number, and we started our little book club and became very close. As I said, she's my best friend."

Liam didn't know what to say. He froze.

"What does this mean, Liam?"

"I don't know, Ivy. But we need to call the detective right away."

Ivy pulled her phone from her pocket and called someone. Liam watched as Ivy waited for whomever she was calling to answer.

"Her phone has been disconnected." Ivy felt panic rise in her throat. She did remember Liam telling her about his high school girlfriend. He said she was crazy. And he had told her the truth.

Liam and Ivy left the clothes he found and their coffee cups in the attic and rushed to find Liam's phone ringing somewhere in the house. Ivy checked the bathroom, and Liam checked the bedroom. He found it just before the call got sent to voicemail.

It was Detective Karnes.

"Hello, this is Liam."

"Liam, are you alone?"

"Yes."

"Can you come down to the station to talk for a minute? Alone."

"I'll be there in five minutes." He rushed out the front door without saying a word to Ivy or the officers talking in the living room.

All the way to the police station, he imagined the worst-case scenarios. He prayed over and over, asking God to keep his kids safe.

It didn't take five minutes; he sped and didn't care.

Officers were waiting outside the station for him in a crowd of people with camera crews. The news was national now. And everyone wanted the details.

The officers escorted him straight back to the detective's office. The station was madness.

"Close the door." Detective Karnes barked.

Liam watched the officer close the door. The detective asked Liam to sit, and after he did so, Detective Karnes laid his arms on the desk in front of him and clasped his hands together.

"What's going on, Detective? You're scaring me. Did you find Scarlett's car? Did you find Ben and Kimber?"

"No, and no. But I have some pretty big questions to ask. And I don't even know where to begin."

Liam leaned forward, anxious to know what the older man sitting across from him was about to say.

"So, to start, we can't find anyone by the name of Tia Gaines. Nowhere. The address Ms. Cameron gave us is an old, condemned shack that hasn't been lived in for years." The detective could see that Liam was feeling sick.

Liam knew why they couldn't find anyone by the name of Tia Gaines. And they never would. "Detective." Liam took a deep breath, leaned forward in his chair, and stared deeply into the detective's worn eyes. "You won't find anyone by the name of Tia Gaines. The woman Ivy was telling you about, her real name is Robin Gaines." Liam cleared his throat, and tears filled his eyes because he knew everything was spiraling out of control. Everything they thought they knew was wrong. "And you won't be able to find her either, because she's dead."

"You're telling me that your ex-wife's best friend, whom she claimed to be having dinner with two nights ago, has died?" The detective was as confused as Liam had been moments earlier in the attic with Ivy.

"She didn't just die. She died the night of our high school graduation. She was my girlfriend, we had been dating for several years, and after graduation, we had a fight that I can't even remember what it was about. Later that night, she died when she used a razor blade to cut her wrists in the bathtub."

The detective leaned back in his chair, and they both sat silently for a moment.

"We spoke to the restaurant staff, and they recalled seeing Ivy that night, but she was alone. We pulled the camera footage, and they were telling the truth. She told us she left the restaurant around 7 o'clock that evening and went straight home, but the babysitter said otherwise. The babysitter states she was paid an extra fifty bucks to stay until midnight. And that Ivy didn't get home until about 12:15 am. We contacted the home security system company, and their records indicate that the home security system went offline as Ivy left for dinner and remained offline with no camera footage or times of the main doors opening or closing."

"Woah. Wait a second. If you are implying that Ivy had anything to do with our kids missing, you're wrong. She's confused and needs to see a doctor. Next, you'll tell me that she kidnapped Scarlett too!" Liam paced back and forth.

The detective didn't reply. Liam's head shot back at him, searching for truth in the detective's eyes, and he froze for the second time this morning.

"We pulled Ivy's phone records. The night before the kids went missing, she made a call to Scarlett at 7:46 pm. They spoke for three minutes and seven seconds. The last time Scarlett's cell pinged from a tower was when she and Ivy were together at Lake Morissette at 8:14 pm. Ivy's phone was untraceable from that moment as well until she called 9-1-1 from the park yesterday morning at 11:27 am."

"Why are you telling me all this?" Liam sat back down. His body was in shock. His mind was spinning.

"I'm telling you all this because we need your help. We want to put a wire on you and have you speak with Ivy. Talk to her in private. Confront her, lie, beg, trick, do whatever you have to do to get the truth, and find out where Ms. Black is and where the children are. Here is a little more evidence that we have collected. He handed him a manilla folder. I'll give you a minute." The detective left his office.

Liam couldn't believe what he was reading. It had happened again, and he had missed it. It happened right in front of him, and he didn't even notice. This time it wasn't a storm. It was a freaking catastrophe. He just read. *No children's footprints present in dirt where the toy truck was located. It appeared to be placed there.* Liam kept reading, his heartbeat pulsating in his fingertips. *A child's training cup was found near the slide, confirmed to belong to missing victim #2 (Kimber Cameron). Testing only showed fingerprints and DNA of the child's mother, Ivy Cameron. No evidence that the child used the cup.* Liam ran his hand through his hair. He was starting to sweat. The kids didn't even go with Ivy to the park that day.

Detective Karnes returned to his office and handed Liam a cold bottle of water. His mouth was bone dry, but he may vomit if he drank anything.

"You mentioned earlier that Ivy and Scarlett were at Lake Morissette, Ivy and I own a boat, and it's docked there. Ivy's boyfriend, Joseph, has the keys because he was interested in buying it."

The detective picked up his phone and made calls ordering officers to locate the boat and continue searching the area. He also wanted to speak with Joseph Pratt.

Twenty minutes later, the door opened, and an officer escorted Joseph inside.

Liam could sense the hate and anger seeping from him the second the door closed, and he laid eyes on Liam.

"Thank you for coming in to talk with us, Mr. Pratt."

"Of course, anything to help Ivy find the kids."

"Really, we just have a couple of questions about the boat. It's my understanding you are considering purchasing the boat from Mr. and Ms. Cameron, is that right?"

"Yes, I was. I'm not now."

"Mr. Cameron states that he gave you the keys to the boat at Ivy's home. Is that true?"

"He did." Joseph refused to look in Liam's direction.

"And do you still have those keys? Have you accessed the boat since that day?"

"What is this about, Liam?" Now he was looking straight at him. "I am so sick of you. First, you cheat on your wife while she is suffering from postpartum depression after having your daughter, then you abandon her and go shack up with the woman she hates most in the world, and while she is recovering from an accident, you let that woman around the kids without permission, you didn't even talk to Ivy about it. And then, when the first opportunity arrives, and she is vulnerable, you have your way with her. Knowing how fragile she is." Joseph stood to his feet and walked over to the door. "You broke her, Liam. Again and again. You are still breaking her." Joseph turned the knob and opened the door. "I never got to go look at the boat; the keys were stolen the night someone broke into Ivy's house." He left the office and then slammed the door behind him.

After all the truth Joseph just spewed all over Liam, his insides shattered. It was all true. He had broken Ivy. The woman he promised to protect, always. They are sitting here today, all because of the choices Liam made time and time again.

But something didn't sit right. It was something he had missed just this morning. The ball cap. His ball cap. The last time he wore it was the day that Scarlett threw it onto the floor next to the bed in the cabin of the boat. He had forgotten it, and it was left on the floor. Ivy must have found it on the boat and taken it back to the house.

"The boat. Ivy may have taken them to the boat." Liam stood as the detective began making calls.

"Liam! The detective called from his office as he was already crossing the station lobby. He stopped, then turned to listen. "Go to Ivy. Now. Not the dock."

Chapter Forty-Five

NOW

Liam wanted to follow the detective's instructions, but his gut told him to drive past town and head east toward the marina. So, he did. Again, he was on autopilot. The steering wheel was turning, the gas pedal was pressed, and he braked at the red lights, but something else was escorting him to the lake. Not himself. He was numb.

He did notice the song playing over the radio, though. And just like that, he wasn't sitting in the truck driving to the lake, praying for his children and Scarlett to be okay. He was driving the boat up the lake. Ivy was by his side, her head on his shoulder, the sun sat high in a cloudless sky, and this same song was playing. The memory had stayed with him and would long after the boat and Ivy was gone. That day he knew deep down he would lose her eventually. Ivy was smiling, staying close to his side, and they were happy, but with the night came the past. When the sun began to settle, so did all the pain. It settled in the space between them as Ivy moved further away from him. So as the song played and the boat created a wake in the placid water, he held on to her tight while he still could.

But the reality was that last night he held a ghost. And he needed to talk to her. He called Ivy, and when she answered, his heart plummeted. He tried not to let his voice crack and to breathe normally. But he was failing. Tears were falling.

"Liam, are you there? Is everything okay? Where did you go?" Ivy's voice was as sweet as the song on the lake that summer day. Sweeter even.

"Ivy, baby," he sobbed, "what did you do?" Liam couldn't follow the detective's instructions on this either. He didn't need to lie, trick or manipulate her. He was sure that she would tell him.

The line grew silent. And the silence was ear-piercing and long.

"Ivy," Liam's voice was raspy this time, like he'd been to a concert the night before.

"Liam," she started to cry, "I'm so sorry."

"Oh God, Ivy."

"I was just going to make you hate Scarlett. It was all Tia's idea to make it look like she wanted to hurt me and that she took the kids. And then it got messy and... I'm sorry, Liam." The line went dead.

"Fuck!" Liam threw the phone onto the floorboard and screamed out. "WHAT DID YOU DO, IVY?!!!!" he screamed over and over.

"This is a newsflash bulletin. In Marion County at Lake Morissette near campsite number thirty-seven, a black four-door sedan was found by police. The owner of the vehicle was last seen by her boyfriend, Liam Cameron, whose children have been missing from Riverside Park since yesterday morning. Mr. Cameron stated that he and Ms. Black had a dispute, and she left two nights ago. It appears that the car was driven into the lake. At this time, we are waiting on the authorities for more information as they are pulling the car from the water. Stay tuned for updates here on Lake 97.4. Your favorite radio station for music, entertainment, and local news."

Liam's phone lying on the black rubber floor mat started ringing, and texts were coming in. He couldn't stop, though. He needed to get to the lake. He had to.

The marina was chaos. His eyes darted around the marina; there were ambulances, fire trucks, rescue vehicles, police cars, water patrol trucks, boats, and news crew vans everywhere.

"I can't allow you to enter; we have an emergency situation." A fireman with thinning grey hair motioned for him to turn around.

"That's my family they are looking for!" Liam wouldn't take no for an answer. Not today.

"Wait here, and I'll radio the sheriff."

Liam threw the truck into *park* without turning off the engine. He needed to find campsite number thirty-seven. He started sprinting. People pointed. Officers called out for him to stop. He ran toward all the chaos until he saw the wrecker truck backed up to the lake. The wench was chained to the back of Scarlett's car. It was covered in mud and debris. Liam ran faster. The front of the car was still submerged under water. Liam couldn't hear anything. But he could see Detective Roberts running from the car toward him. His arms were out in front of him, and his hands were waving for him to stop. Liam wasn't stopping. Liam would tackle him if he needed to.

"Liam, stop! Wait!" The detective ordered. "Can I get some help over here?! Now!" Four more officers joined the detective, grabbing Liam and tackling him onto the ground. "Are they in there?! Are my kids dead?!" Liam was screaming. Dirt and dust filled his eyes and mouth as he wrestled the officers with all he had.

"Liam, stop. You shouldn't be here. Please calm down," Detective Roberts regained his composure and caught his breath.

Liam stopped fighting. He saw the empathy in the detective's eyes. Liam thought he might vomit.

"Listen to me, Liam. I don't know about the kids yet. But they think that Scarlett Black is inside the vehicle."

Liam couldn't speak. His mouth wouldn't move. This can't be happening.

"If you will just stay here with the officers and let me go do my job, I'll come back and tell you what I find as soon as we can get inside the car. Okay? Are you listening to me?" Detective Roberts was out of breath.

Liam sobbed. The detective motioned for the officers to release him, and Liam sat up, pulled his knees to his chest, covered his face with his hands, and sobbed.

"Stay with him." The officers nodded in unison that they understood.

Liam turned to face the water. It was a beautiful summer day. Just like the one he had just been thinking about in the truck moments ago. Whatever love and endearment he had felt for Ivy was long gone. As the car was dragged further and further out of the lake, hate and more hate ate up whatever love for Ivy he had. He thought of the way Scarlett had carefully brushed Kimber's hair that first night they met one another. He recalled how she held the syrup bottle and let Ben wrap his hands around hers to help pour the warm brown syrup over his pancakes. Ben was so proud.

Lastly, he remembered the way she loved himself. The way she forgave him, the way she made him better. Liam prayed. And he prayed. And he prayed some more. Begging, bargaining, whatever he needed to do. The car was out, and water poured out onto the gravel and dirt. Liam ran. He ran past the four officers, the firefighters, and the rescue workers. He was like a running back trying his hardest to get the football to the goal line. Like his whole life depended on it.

That's when he could see it. He stopped dead in his tracks. He didn't want to take one step closer. In fact, he fell and began crawling backward, scurrying, grabbing onto whatever he could to help him.

He couldn't see a lot. But he saw strawberry blonde hair trapped in the closed passenger side door.

His eyes locked with Detective Roberts, and he heard him speak into his radio. "Is this Officer Tim at the Cameron residence? Over."

"This is Tim on sight, sir. Over."

"Place Ivy Cameron under arrest and escort her straight to the station. Over."

Silence.

"Officer Tim, did you hear me? That is a direct order. Over."

"Um, Sir, Ivy Cameron left the residence earlier today, and she has not returned. Over."

"Damn it!" The detective kicked the large, rusted trash can.

"Attention, this is Detective Roberts. Please put out an APB for Ivy Cameron. She's wanted for possible murder and considered armed and dangerous. Over."

Chapter Forty-Six

TWO DAYS AGO

This is so stupid. Scarlett thought as she drove away from the only man she had ever loved over something so trivial. She was being selfish, childish, and unreasonable. She knew it, but she was mad. Earlier this afternoon, she was hurt and furious. Seeing Ivy and Liam together, having a picnic with the kids, was difficult. She wanted them to co-parent, but this looked like so much more. She knew Liam would always care for his ex-wife. She knew at the end of the day that their marriage had ended because Ivy wanted it that way. Not Liam. But she and Liam had begun building a life together. He told her he loved her. She was living with him. She had the opportunity to hold and care for his children in hopes that someday, she may become important to them in the way they were already important to her. I mean, isn't that what love is, after all? Being important to one another?

If she was important to Liam, wouldn't he care if this hurt her? Wouldn't he understand she had the right to be a little insecure and jealous? Just a little.

Scarlett had no clue where she was going or how she would swallow her pride and go back home to Liam, but she would. Eventually. First, she needed to calm down, and then she needed to find the words to make him understand that what he did today was disrespectful. He could go to Ivy and the kids when they needed him. But not like that. Not a picnic.

The cell phone lying in the passenger seat vibrated. It was Liam. She refused to answer. She wasn't ready to speak to him; she was still too mad and hurt.

A minute later, she listened to his voicemail.

Hey baby, it's Liam. He paused and then sighed. *I'm sorry. You're right. Today was unnecessary. I should have left once the alarm company arrived. It was inconsiderate to you. And I want you to know that... you are my family. I love you. I have for longer than you know. I'm thankful for everything you have put up with. I'll do better. I choose you. I'm all in. You and me. I promise. Come home. Bye.*

He said all the words she needed him to say. All the cracks in her heart from earlier that day were mending. She swallowed hard and wiped tears from her face.

Her phone vibrated again when she was about to make a U-turn. She would answer Liam's call this time. But the person calling wasn't Liam. Her heart sank a little. Ivy has never called or messaged her, ever. She didn't want to answer, but she knew she should. What if Ivy needed something? What if the kids were sick or hurt? Scarlett hates that Ivy will always have the upper hand, but if that means she gets Liam, then Ivy can have all the power within the boundaries she plans on making very clear soon.

"Hello?" Scarlett listened; she waited for Ivy to say something. "Hello?" she repeated.

"Scarlett?" Ivy sounded a little upset. Her voice was low and different from the day on the street at the farmer's market.

"Yeah? Is everything okay?"

"Everything is fine. I've just left dinner with a friend, the kids are at home with the sitter, and I know it's late, but could you meet me? To talk. Just the two of us, I mean. I know things are starting to get serious between you and Liam and that you are spending time with the kids now, and I just thought we should talk."

Scarlett hesitated. She wanted to say *no* and suggest that they meet another time. But she also wanted to discuss a few things with Liam's ex-wife in person.

"Of course. I'm actually just heading back home now, but I can meet you. Where?" Scarlett didn't want to sound like a jealous girlfriend, but she was.

"I have to make a quick stop at Lake Morissette and drop off the boat keys in the drop box at the marina for a prospective buyer who wants to look at the boat tomorrow morning. Would you be able to meet there?"

"I can be there in a few minutes." Scarlett rolled her eyes.

"Great. See you then."

She started to message Liam and tell him that she was going to meet his ex-wife but decided not to involve him. He would worry and probably interfere. Why bother him? She'd talk to Ivy for fifteen minutes and then go straight home. She might not even tell Liam they spoke. She will go inside the house, strip off all her clothes, and have incredible make up sex. There's no reason to bring Ivy into the rest of the night. She got enough of Liam earlier that day.

Chapter Forty-Seven

TWO DAYS AGO

Ivy was nervous. But she was also determined to say everything she wanted to say to Scarlett. And talk about boundaries. For example, whether Liam is at his ex-wife's house or not, she was to stay off her street. She doesn't get to drive by and intrude on their time together.

Stay calm. Don't cry. Don't let her hurt you any more than she already has. She got Liam because you let him go. Ivy wasn't entirely certain if that last part was true.

She lied. She didn't need to drop off keys to the marina. She had left the restaurant upset and didn't want to go home and asked the babysitter to stay a little later for some extra money. She didn't want to do the kid's nighttime routine this evening. She was hurting, and she wanted to keep that from them. She just needed a little time to herself. She remembered the boat keys she had in her purse. She had lied to Joseph that night. She told him they had been stolen. But she had hidden them. She didn't want him to buy the boat. What if she and Liam get back together? They love this boat. It belongs to them. They had made love for hours many times on both the top deck hidden in a cove and down inside the cabin. And perhaps one day, they would want to be together in that way again. No, she won't be selling the boat.

But as she came aboard and wandered down into the cabin, she knew. She could feel it in her veins. Ivy wasn't the only woman Liam made love to on their boat. She could almost see them together, there in their special place. Ivy touched the slightly disheveled comforter, and it was as if the truth slapped her across the face. The skin on her cheek burned with pain. Something on the floor between the bed and the wall caught her eye. It was Liam's ball cap. When she touched it, something kicked the breath out of her. She grabbed ahold of her middle section. She couldn't breathe. Something invisible was there with her, slapping her, kicking her. Like a ghost. Like rage.

Fury overcame her. Hate-filled her heart, almost to the point that she wasn't sure she even had one anymore. That's okay; she didn't need it anyway. It had already been damaged beyond repair.

The organ in her chest turned black and shriveled into something much different than the heart she was born with. It was ugly and dark. Evil maybe. When your heart becomes this way, you are capable of almost anything. *Scary*, she thought. But worth it. She wanted Scarlett's face to be as black as the thing in her chest barely beating. She lowered herself onto the bed slowly, pressing the ball cap against her skin. Closing her eyes, she laid back onto the comforter and pulled the cap to her face. It smelled like her ex-husband. It reminded her of his laundry she folded fresh out of the dryer. It smelled like his t-shirt that she would wear after they made love sometimes. She could cry. She could even probably lay there and die. That's how badly this hurt. But she shouldn't be the one to hurt. It should be Scarlett.

Liam would hate Ivy if she hurt her. But what if Scarlett hurt the things Liam loved most in this world? Then he would hate her. Not Ivy. He would hate her so much that he would want to kill her too.

Ivy needed to think fast. She didn't have a lot of time. She placed Liam's ball cap on her head and straightened her dark hair. Then she dialed the numbers. She wanted to snap her fingers and Scarlett be there already. She wanted to fight. She wanted Scarlett to hurt as she had.

The line rang once, then twice, three times… "Hello?"

Ivy's SUV was parked near the tree line. The marina was closed. Everything was dark. On the weekends in the summer, this place is busy beyond belief. But on a weeknight, it's isolated. Ivy began walking slowly toward the marina through the parking lot in hopes that once Scarlett arrived, she would join her. Seconds later, headlights approached. It was Scarlett's black Audi. Ivy's twisted dead heart skipped a beat. She stopped, squeezing the boat keys in her hand.

Scarlett parked beside Ivy's SUV and got out of her car. She wasn't surprised that Liam had chosen Scarlett. She was beautiful. He liked tall, curvy women. And this one was smart, successful, and probably great in bed. But the strawberry blonde hair had always confused her a little. Liam obsessed over Ivy's straight black hair. The whole time they were together, she made sure to keep it silky and long. Just the way he liked. The girlfriends he had before her all were dark-haired as well. And she doubts that Ms. Scarlett has any tattoos. Liam helped Ivy choose all of hers. He even went and held her hand. Then sometimes at night, he ran his fingers over them while she lay in his arms. Tracing them, one by one. Touching his lips to her skin. She loved him more for it.

"I have to take this key down to the marina drop box at the main office. Walk with me? And then we can get out of here. I've got to get back to the sitter." Ivy pretended to look down at the watch on her wrist, concerned.

Scarlett didn't reply, but she beeped her alarm, stuffed her hands in her jeans pockets, and walked toward her.

She smells like Liam. Ivy squeezed the boat key so tightly in her hand that she knew she broke the skin.

Even after they walked for a minute through the parking lot, no one said anything. Ivy was about to break the silence when Scarlett stopped walking, removed her hands from her pockets, and crossed her arms over her chest.

"I know the games you play, Ivy. Liam doesn't see it. But I do."

Surprised by the tone and initiation, Ivy was taken aback. She stopped and turned to the woman who smelled of her ex-husband's aftershave.

"Excuse me? What games are you referring to, Scarlett?" Ivy followed suit and crossed her arms over her chest as well.

"Don't play innocent, Ivy. Stop. Let's just be real for a minute. Stop the bullshit. Liam isn't here. So just say what you really want to say."

"You don't get to speak to me like this." Ivy wasn't used to being confrontational. The entire time she and Liam were together after his affair, Ivy never called Scarlett out, not once. She never caused drama. And when she learned that he was with her after the divorce, Ivy stayed clear of the two of them. But now, she was raging inside, and she let the tarry, melted thing in her chest cavity take over. She let the evil take her soul.

"That night, after I told Liam to leave, I searched for him. I wanted to tell him that I didn't mean it. I looked everywhere for him… but your arms. It rained and rained that weekend. I thought it would never stop. I cried just as much. And then Sunday came. And Liam came home. And it was still raining."

"What's your point, Ivy?"

Ivy took a few steps closer to Scarlett. "The point is that I want you to know what he said to me. I want you to know what he's always said to me about you."

Ivy watched Scarlett smirk and then roll her eyes. "He told me that you are the biggest regret of his entire life, that every part of you felt like disgust when he was with you. He said that if he could take back anything in this world… it would be the first time he touched you."

"I don't have to listen to this." Scarlett threw her arms in the air and started back toward her car.

"Yes! You do." Ivy jumped in front of her, cutting her off. "You had an affair with my husband, Scarlett. So yes, you have to hear what I want to say to you!" Ivy watched Scarlett's eyes grow wide and her body tense. "The only reason he's with you right now is because I was the one who filed for divorce. I'm the one who told him to leave and never come back. And you know what?" Ivy was now only inches from Scarlett's face. "He's gotten down onto his knees and begged me. Begged to come home. He's told me, over and over, I… not you… am the love of his life. So, let's get one thing clear. I don't play games. I'm just the ex-wife you screwed over. I'm always going to be the mother of his children, Scarlett. And he's always going to love me more. So, as I said, I don't need to play any games. If you are so insecure and jealous of me that you have to leave work in the middle of the day to drive down my street and past my house to check on Liam, then I think it's you that needs to come up with some games to play. And no matter what, you will always be the one who will lose when the game is against me."

"You're crazy. You were crazy after you had the kids, and you are still crazy." Scarlett moved even closer to Ivy's face. They were nearly nose to nose. "That's what Liam said to me… about you."

Ivy's hand raised high and slapped Scarlett's face as hard as whatever invisible ghost had slapped Ivy on the boat moments earlier.

Scarlett's mouth opened wide as she touched her cheek. "I'm done. I can't wait to tell Liam about this."

Ivy let her get just steps away from her car door before she reared back the rock she had picked up by the tree seconds earlier and then slammed it into the back of Scarlett's head. Scarlett screamed out in pain and fear. Ivy hit her again. This time she hit her temple. Scarlett fell onto the blacktop. Ivy watched as the woman covered her head with her hands, scurrying toward her car, crying out. Ivy let her be afraid. She let her wet herself. She let her look everywhere in the darkness for Liam, who wasn't there to save her. She hit her again. The blood poured down her face, her eyes closed, and the crying stopped. Ivy kneeled beside her, breathed in her ex-husband's cologne one last time… then smiled.

Chapter Forty-Eight

NOW

"Liam. Liam! Listen to me. It's not her. It's not Scarlett."

Liam's head raised. He looked at Detective Roberts and then toward the car. He watched as a gloved investigator placed a strawberry blonde wig inside a clear plastic evidence bag and sealed it.

"No one was inside the car, Liam."

Liam took a deep breath and thanked God.

"Did you check the boat?" Liam had a difficult time adjusting to the sunlight. He used his hand to shield his eyes as he spoke to the detective. Detective Karnes had arrived at some point and was standing next to Detective Roberts.

"We tried, but the boat isn't in its slip. The marina is pulling the camera footage. We should know something soon. We've also got the rescue teams and water patrol searching the lake."

"I could go to Ivy and get her to tell me exactly where they are, and she..."

Detective Karnes interrupted Liam. "That won't work. Ivy's gone. She left the house after you did this morning when I asked you to come down to the station. No one has seen her since. We have units looking for her."

"I want to help. I know the lake. Ivy only knows the places I have taken her to. I can show you!" Liam stood and started walking back toward the marina. His suit pants were covered in dirt and dust from the gravel. His white button-up was drenched with sweat.

"Soon. Let's get that footage first and get you something to drink." The two detectives walked with him back to the marina, where a tent was set up for shade to sit and computers. It was a meeting station for everyone doing everything possible to help find Scarlett, Ben, and Kimber. And now Ivy.

Liam passed the shelter and went straight to the shower house. It was empty. He was alone. He locked the door, undressed, and stepped beneath the water. He didn't know if the water was hot or cold. He was numb. Inside and out. He just needed a minute. A minute to process what was happening. Everything would be different now. Forever. Once they find the kids, Ivy will never come near them again. They have lost their mom. He will never go near her again. He couldn't. He hates her too much. Even if they are alive, he hates her. And he always will.

Chapter Forty-Nine

TWO DAYS AGO

"Tia, I need your help," Ivy's voice trembled. Her entire body was shaking uncontrollably.

"Oh, God, Ivy. What did you do?"

"Help me. Please." Ivy cried into the phone.

"I'm on my way." The line went dead.

It's what every best friend says when the other is in trouble. And Ivy was certainly in trouble. She had taken everything too far. She had slipped. She didn't mean to.

Ivy paced back and forth around Scarlett, lying on the ground, bleeding. Not moving. The large, jagged rock was still safe and sound in her right hand, covered in Scarlett's red blood. Should she throw it into the trees, hide it in her car, and toss it into the lake as she crosses the bridge? She pondered as she paced. She would wait on Tia. Tia would know what to do.

"Oh, Ivy." Ivy turned to see her friend. She was so happy she came.

"It's bad, Tia. What am I going to do?"

Tia looked around the marina for anyone who might be watching them but saw no one. They were alone. "Is she alive?" Tia asked.

"I don't know," Ivy whispered.

Tia lowered herself onto the ground beside the woman lying so still that she could be mistaken for a mannequin. She lay next to her, trying to be just as still, just as silent, just as dead. But the task was impossible. Tia reached out to move a strand of hair away from her face to see her eyes. She wondered if they were open. It would be difficult to tell in the dark, but she needed to see. Closed; her eyes are closed. Disappointment swirled inside her. "We need to move her. Now! Before someone sees us."

"I can't," Ivy took a few steps back, shaking her head back and forth with her arms tightly crossed over her chest.

"You have to, Ivy."

Reluctantly, Ivy stepped forward and grabbed ahold of her ex-husband's new love. She isn't new, though, is she? She's been around causing problems for a while now. Ivy held her calves as tightly as she could, dragging her toward the boat. Blood dripped from Scarlett's head. Ivy hadn't noticed until they reached the water and stepped onto the dock's wooden planks. She watched them fall. Drip. Drip. Drip.

"Don't worry about it. We'll get a bucket and clean it up on the way back." Tia led Ivy straight to "Dance With Me".

Once they locked Scarlett inside the boat's cabin, they used lake water and the old bucket on the dock to rinse away the drops of blood they had left behind. Ivy also dipped her hands into the dark water and let the red liquid shed away as if it had never been on her skin at all.

Ivy drove Scarlett's car home and parked it discreetly in the garage, hoping no one would notice. When Ivy inserted the key into the front door, then stepped inside her home, panic settled in her throat. She spoke carefully to Lacy; less is more in situations like this. Saying too much can get you into trouble; it can get you caught. The annoyed, pimply-faced adolescent quietly gathered her things and left with her extra cash.

The house fell silent as she waited on Tia to come inside and save the day. Ivy let her hand drag up the honey-colored wooden handrail as she slowly walked up the stairs in the darkness. She didn't need light to show her the way to Kimber's bedroom. She could smell her baby girl as soon as she pushed the door open. All her senses calmed. She just needed to see her, and then she would know everything would be okay, and they would get through this night. But, when she reached her daughter's bed, Kimber was screaming. She was shaking her blood-covered face side to side frantically. The car seat strap was still securely in place, but shards of glass were all over her.

"Shhh, it's okay, baby girl. Mama's here now," Ivy couldn't console the infant. Just as she tried to clear the glass away, she heard Ben down the hall. He was crying out for her. "Mommy, wake up!" She slammed open his bedroom door only to be greeted by silence. The sounds of her breathing and panicking were the only sounds in the whole house. She rushed over to the little boy sleeping peacefully in his bed. She turned and ran back to her daughter's bedside to find her sleeping just the same. Ivy had slipped. She slipped back to the night she drove straight for that tree. The rain was pouring down, her heart was breaking, and that tree held all the answers and peace she needed... they needed. Guilt choked her, and vomit spewed from her lips. It took only seconds to reach the toilet and hover over it. After five minutes of retching, she felt her stomach start to relax. Then she noticed the dried red blood all over her hands and arms. It was Scarlett Black's blood. The stains seeping into her pores belonged to her ex-husband's mistress. She felt vomit rising again. How had she not noticed the blood earlier? How had Tia not noticed? Oh, no. What if Lacy noticed?

Running over to the bathroom sink, she rubbed the white bar of soap and scorching hot water over her hands and arms. Her skin was stained red, and she couldn't remove it. She grabbed the toilet brush from the container on the floor, doused the tinged bristles with bleach and hot water, and then scraped her skin hard. She screamed out as she moved the brush harder and harder.

"Ivy! What are you doing?! Stop!" Tia grabbed the brush and turned off the steaming hot water.

"Her blood is all over me and won't come off. Is it on my face?!" Ivy's eyes, full of madness, searched her reflection in the bathroom mirror. "I think it got into my mouth and eyes!"

"Shhh! Stop, Ivy. There's no blood anywhere! You're going to wake the kids." Tia held both of Ivy's red, scratched arms in her hands tightly.

Ivy opened her eyes and scoured her reflection once more. Tia was telling the truth. There wasn't a drop of Scarlett's blood on her anywhere.

"You've got to pull it together, Ivy," Tia whispered as she pulled Ivy close and lowered her onto the cold tile floor beside her. "We are going to get you out of these wet clothes, and then you need to listen very carefully to every word I say. If you don't, your life is over. You will go to prison forever and never see your kids again. Do you understand me, Ivy?"

"I can't lose my kids, Tia." Ivy's eyes filled with tears. "I didn't mean to hurt her, I got so angry, and I just blacked out. When I came to, there she was on the blacktop. She was bleeding, and when I said her name, she didn't move. I'm sorry. Please, don't let me lose my babies." The tears fell as she clung to her friend, begging for help.

"I told you a long time ago you needed to let Liam go," Tia stroked at Ivy's long dark hair.

"I know you did. But I want him. I want him to be mine again, Tia. I can't live without him."

"I think we can fix this. I have a plan. One that I think will give you everything you want. What do you want, Ivy?" Tia whispered, still stroking Ivy's long black hair.

Ivy's sobbing slowed, and her breathing steadied, "I want Liam to hate her. I want him to wish she was dead. And I want him to want me. I want him only to love me." Whatever weak piece of her that made her slip just now was gone, and all the darkness that filled her up back at the lake was back, and it was angrier and stronger.

Tia smiled, greeting her friend's darkness with her own. "If you want Liam to hate Scarlett and you want her gone forever, she has to hurt him. What would hurt Liam most in this world, Tia? What does he love more than you?"

"He loves the kids," Ivy whispered.

"Very good, Ivy. He does love the kids very much. We can make it look like Scarlett tried to hurt the kids, and then she has to die. Listen to me, Ivy." Tia touched her forehead to Ivy's, and they looked into one another's eyes. "This will be risky. We can't let the kids know it's us taking them."

"Where are we taking them?" Ivy listened closely for her friend to reply.

"We will take them to the boat, Ivy. They will be with Scarlett, and then we will go back for them before it sinks. But when the time comes, and the boat goes down, Scarlett has to go with it, or she'll tell Liam the truth. She'll ruin everything. But do you know what this means, Ivy?" she whispered to her inside the dark house.

Ivy was crying quietly; she couldn't speak. "It means you will be a murderer. Do you understand what I'm saying to you?" Tia spoke clearly for her to hear.

Ivy shook her head up and down, saying yes.

"And you have to take this secret with you to the grave. You can't ever tell anyone what we are about to do. Never."

"I'll take this secret to the grave. I promise I'll never tell."

The fake strawberry blonde hair itched Ivy's scalp. It was hot. She felt beads of sweat on her forehead. "Shhh, it's okay. Your daddy will come be with us soon. Keep your eyes closed."

Ivy held on to Ben's hand as she walked with Kimber on her hip.

"Where are we going, Scarlett?"

"Remember what I told you in the car? It's a surprise. You can look when we get there. Keep your eyes closed."

The little boy with Liam's eyes stumbled as he stepped onto the wooden dock.

"We're almost there." She whispered as the night bugs sang into the summer night.

They reached the slip, and Ivy helped them aboard. She didn't turn on any lights and did everything Tia said.

"We are on the boat!" Ben jumped up and down as Kimber sucked on her passy; her eyes were still half awake and half asleep.

"Yes, we are. Now let's lay on the bed and go back to sleep. When the sun wakes up, we will wake up. Okay?" She helped them pull the covers up to their chins, and they snuggled close.

Ivy tried not to cry. "I'll be back, I promise." She kissed their foreheads and locked them inside.

She had watched Liam do this a million times. She carefully untied the rope from the dock and eased the boat out of the slip. She knew exactly where to go. Liam had taken her to a cove once. It felt like you had to coast for days to get to the end, but you could see an old mill once you arrived. It was overgrown and difficult to see, but it was there. There is a mile-long narrow path back to the marina from the mill. Tia promised she would be waiting for me in the cove at the mill on the bank.

She gently eased onto the throttle after she left the No Wake Zone. The night air was humid, but the breeze mixing with sprays of lake water felt like heaven against Ivy's skin. Ivy thought about her children down below with Scarlett, and her heart sank. She considered turning around and calling the police, but then she remembered the sweet promises of what would come after this. She imagined her, Liam, and the kids together again. His hand in hers. His lips kissing her the way he used to. She snapped back to reality and slowed the boat as she entered the cove. The darkness was so thick it was as if the moon knew what Ivy was up to and refused to shine down on her. She felt the ghost so close behind her as she gripped the steering wheel; she couldn't breathe. Fear stole the air from her lungs. She feared it would toss her into the lake, and she would drown. She choked back the feeling of the ghost and focused on driving the boat. She could barely see if any debris was in the way. Finally, she reached the end of the cove, and Tia was there just like she promised.

She dropped the anchors, used ropes to tie off between trees, and then she was in the water, swimming toward the bank, toward her friend, leaving Ben and Kimber behind.

They walked quickly, hand in hand, and didn't look back. They didn't stop to see if it was an animal or the ghost from the boat following close behind. Ivy pulled off the wig and let her scalp breathe. She dropped the strawberry blonde hair but stopped to pick it up quickly. She was thankful Tia had the wig for her to use. Finally, they reached the marina, and no one saw a thing.

The ride home was full of instructions from Tia; Ivy listened hard to every single one. She had turned off all the cameras and security system earlier that day. She hadn't really wanted one, but she let Liam do whatever made him feel better. And she got to spend the day with him. So, she guessed that if she had played a game today, she won.

She and Tia slept very little, then prepared a picnic basket, received her delivery of pale pink roses, and headed to Riverside Park. All the things she had planned to do anyway. It was her and Liam's wedding anniversary. But Scarlett ruined everything. She had to smell like Liam, and she had to say those things.

Ivy used a back road into the park and left using the busy highway, knowing that someone needed to see a strawberry-blonde-haired woman driving Scarlett's car away from the park at this time.

She drove quickly back to the marina. The campground had two sides. One for campers and one for primitive camping. Only a few people camp in tents these days. Lucky for Ivy, no one was this morning. So, she let Tia out of the car and drove it into the lake. She jumped out and shut the door before the car reached the bank and touched the water. Ivy waited and watched it sink. The water bubbled. It took longer than she thought it would. But she waited anyway. She wished Scarlett had been inside. Never to be seen again. *Soon,* Ivy thought as the car was completely submerged under water. She would always remember campsite number thirty-seven.

They rushed back to Ivy's car, took the backway into the park, then carefully placed Ben's truck on the dirt mound and Kimber's half-full sippy cup with butterflies on the ground next to her favorite slide. They have to help her up the steps, but she always laughs when she or Liam catches her at the bottom.

Exhaustion and adrenaline were one of the same today. Ivy didn't let her aching body slow her down; she kept following Tia's instructions, thankful she was helping her.

"Okay, we're almost at the finish line. Are you ready?" Tia asked.

"I'm ready," Ivy squeezed her eyes shut, anticipating the pain about to radiate through her body. They had to hurry; the playground would get busy soon. And then she felt it. The same rock covered in Scarlett's blood now had Ivy's on it as well.

Ivy fell. She couldn't hear the river flowing because of the bells ringing in her ears. Racing against time, she stumbled over to the river and tossed the rock into the water. It would never see the light of day again, then crawled back to the bench, dialed 9-1-1, and said everything Tia told her to say. Then she closed her eyes and slept.

Chapter Fifty

NOW

Ivy parked at the Jackson Trail starting point near the marina to access the path many don't know is there. It leads down to the old mill by the lake. She hurried as fast as she could. She would get the kids, and they would go. She had removed all the cash from the safe and packed Ben's hard-shelled suitcase with tractors and an oversized diaper bag for Kimber. They'd leave this place and never come back, hiding somewhere no one, not even Liam, could ever find them. But first, she knew she had to make sure Scarlett didn't make it. She had to follow Tia's plan.

Time was running out. The sun was getting overtaken by dark clouds. The leaves on the trees stood straight up toward the sky as the branches swayed in the heavy wind. A storm was coming fast, and she needed to be faster.

Even in the daylight, dark clouds or not, this part of the forest is scary. Ivy looked back to make sure Tia was following close behind her. And she was.

They reached the water. The boat was barely moving. One of the ropes had come unfastened from the tree, but the anchors had stayed secure. Ivy was proud of herself.

Ivy removed her sandals in the grass where she could find them when she swims back, then walked to the water's edge. The water teased her toes, inviting her in.

"It's okay; I'll be right by your side the whole time. Just remove the plug; you know how. Then get the kids, make sure Scarlett is locked in, and we will swim back. Easy peasy."

"Easy peasy," Ivy whispered as she stepped into the water and swam toward the boat.

She knew she didn't have much time once the plug was pulled. And she was right. By the time she got to the cabin door, the boat was taking on water.

"Mama!" Ben grabbed onto Ivy's leg. Then she saw Scarlett grab him and pull him back inside the cabin.

"Give him to me, Scarlett," Ivy stepped inside the stuffy room, "he's mine."

Not obeying Ivy's demand, Scarlett grabbed Kimber, who was sitting on the floor eating a peanut butter cracker. "I said give them to me!" Ivy grabbed at Ben's arm, and he cried out in terror.

Ivy fell as the boat jerked. It was happening. Water was coming into the cabin. Horror filled Scarlett's eyes. She rushed the kids to the door and set them on the top deck.

But as she tried to join them, Ivy grabbed her hair and pulled her back inside. Scarlett turned and punched her hard in the face. Stunned, Ivy fell into the rising water. Scarlett moved fast. Ivy got closer to them as Scarlett instructed Ben to hold tight to her no matter what while she held on to Kimber and swam to the shore.

"Scarlett! They're my kids!" Ivy was struggling. The boat's pressure pulled her under as she clawed for anything to help her out of the cabin.

"Not anymore," Scarlett replied.

Ivy found the top step and pushed hard off the boat. The same bubbles she watched earlier as Scarlett's car sank were now all around her. Ivy made it out. She was safe! All she had to do was swim to the bank to Ben and Kimber!

Suddenly, like in a scene from a horror movie, she felt something grab ahold of her foot and pull her under. Ivy kicked and fought but didn't know what monster was taking her under the lake. The dark clouds had filled the sky, and the rain began to fall so hard that when Ivy's face went above the water, she felt the raindrops sting her skin.

She was growing tired. Her arms were heavy from treading water, from trying to find anything to save her. She saw Scarlett not far ahead. She was going under too. Ivy could help her. She could fix all of this. She could save Scarlett, Ben, and Kimber. But then she couldn't see her anymore. This time when whatever was beneath the water pulled her under, she kept her eyes open to see what it was. There in the deep, placid water, was Tia. She was the monster. Ivy stopped fighting. Her arms quit flailing, and her legs went still. She closed her eyes and let Tia and the lake take her.

Chapter Fifty-One

NOW

The world looks very different during the wrath of a storm. The lake was no longer calm, and the sun no longer pierced Liam's eyes. The rescue boat skidded across the top of the choppy water. Every now and then, they hit a current just right, and the boat would go air born, then slam down back onto the top of the water. Nearly knocking them all overboard. But they couldn't slow down. It didn't matter that the lightning was striking and the thunder was rolling. They needed to search every cove. And they did. The last would be the one with the old mill at the end. Liam directed the boat captain where to turn. They coasted as the boat tried to stay straight in the wind. Darkness had fallen. The lights on the boat shined around them, ahead, and into the water. What an eerie thing to see, Liam thought as he imagined everything that lay on the bottom of the lake. He started to imagine Scarlett and the kids down there and nearly lost it over the side of the boat. He redirected his attention forward, focusing hard and squinting to see the end.

The darkness hid the mill, but he noticed the rope hanging from the tree. Detective Karnes, the captain, two water rescue divers, and himself fell silent as their eyes darted around the cove. Debris floated around them, things Liam recognized from the boat. He wanted to dive into the dark water and look for them. He took a step and felt hands all over him. "Liam, don't." Detective Karnes begged with worried eyes. "It's too late. We're too late."

"No." Liam shook his head back and forth, saying it over and over again. "Scarlett?! He screamed. Then he listened, his eyes skimming the water. "Ben?! Kimber?!" He paused again. Waiting to hear them cry out to him. Nothing. He looked at the other's expressions; they looked at him with pity and sadness like a dead man lying on the street. "Help me! We can still try to find them!" Liam pushed the detective off of him, and the boat rocked.

"Get us out of here!" The detective ordered the captain.

The captain turned the key, and the engine sputtered. "Ben! Scarlett! Kimber!" Liam screamed at the top of his lungs. He's lost everything; he might as well jump in and be with them.

The motor caught, fired up, then died again. Thankfully the wind was starting to calm, the rain changed from large hard drops to a slight mist, and fog settled on top of the water, hiding the floating debris. Everything went silent and calm, but there was no peace. Liam's heart was still racing, and he could tell by the look on Detective Karnes's face that he had given up, not for the night, but for forever. He believed that the kids and Scarlett were dead.

And Liam should believe it too.

The boat ride back was like a dark and twisted, nightmarish memory. How many times had he and Ivy treaded this water with the kids? And alone, just the two of them? How many times had they stopped and dropped anchor to swim? He could still see Kimber wearing her small purple life jacket, splashing in the water as Ivy held onto her. Liam was crying again. Detective Karnes sat close, his hand patting him on the back, trying to offer comfort while desperately trying not to cry himself in front of Liam. But he could cry; Liam didn't mind. Liam didn't know much anymore, but he knew he'd cry every single day for the rest of his life.

Liam was in shock. The boat pulled up to the dock, and one of the guys on board secured the rope, and everyone got off the boat except for Liam and the detective, who was still at his side.

"Liam, let's go get you dry, okay? Get yourself something to drink and a little rest. We will go back out in the morning and pick up where we left off. Okay?"

Like that day at the park, Liam stared at all the firefighters, rescue workers, officers, and first responders. All their lights were flashing, but it was quiet. No sirens made a sound, and everyone was still. No one was rushing around searching or using their phones and radios. Everyone and everything was just still, including Liam. He couldn't move. And when he tried, his knees had given up on him, and he went down. The boat rocked from side to side against the dock as his eyes closed and darkness invaded every piece of his being. He begged God never to let his eyes open again.

Chapter Fifty-Two

EARLIER THAT NIGHT

Lights flickering from the sinking boat danced around the cove and beneath the water. Scarlett could see just enough to know which way to swim to reach the closest bank. The dark water was deep, and the kids were heavy as they clung to her for dear life. She gave every tread and every kick everything she had.

The splashing in the water behind her sounded mad. Ivy resembled a screaming animal desperate to live. Scarlett didn't look back. The flashing lights grew dim as she focused on the rocks and dirt ahead.

"Mama!" Ben called out. His fingers dug into the skin on Scarlett's neck. She didn't have enough air in her lungs, energy, or time to console or comfort him. She was trying to save the three of them from his mama. But how could he ever understand that?

Her feet touched mud that felt like quicksand. She feared they wouldn't make it. The edge of the bank was further than she thought. Water filled Ben's mouth as he cried out for his mother, begging Scarlett to help her. Scarlett wasn't sure she would save Ivy, even if she could.

The flickering stopped. The splashing stopped. Scarlett was certain she couldn't make it any further with the children, they were going to drown, and they were so close. But she felt sharp algae-covered rocks that cut her feet as her one free hand clawed into the moss on the bank.

Once on land, she hurried away from the water as if some kind of monster from a child's nightmare or scary movie was after them and would drag them back. The truth was, she was right. There was a monster in the water. The most dangerous kind. Scarlett pulled the kids close as her panting slowed. Raindrops mixed with hail stung their flesh. But no one made a sound. They just listened. Listened for the monster. Scarlett's eyes were trying to adjust to the darkness. What little bit of moonlight coming from the stormy sky helped her see that the water had become still. The boat and everything in it had sunk to the bottom of the lake, taking the monster with it.

"We have to go." Scarlett's throat burned. It sounded like she was whispering, but she wasn't. The kids had fallen silent, probably from shock. Kimber was still holding on tight to her neck, and Ben was squeezing her hand so hard she thought it might fall off. But she just kept putting one foot in front of the other. She didn't look back. Rocks, leaves, and twigs ripped at her cold and wet skin. Spider webs stuck to her face and hair, but she kept moving. She didn't know where she was going but knew that cliffs and dangerous terrains were nearby. She would get them a little further from the lake, and then they would find a place out of the rain until the sun came back to save them.

Five more minutes passed, and the rain was only falling harder. Lightning flashed across the dark sky, and thunder crashed all around them. Scarlett kept her eyes open wide and waited for one more lightning strike. As soon as it did, her eyes darted everywhere, searching for anything that would give them cover. Thankfully there was a cliffside to their left. She, Ben, and Kimber crouched beneath a large boulder and held on to one another as if the world was falling apart. She knew in their little hearts, it was.

Every time Scarlett's eyes closed, and sleep found her, so did Ivy. She would jerk awake and nearly scream out. Even in the summer, the night was cold. Their three bodies shivered and shook. Scarlett couldn't pull them closer to her, as she was already holding them as tightly as she could.

Then the rain stopped, just like the splashing behind her in the lake had. The lightning stopped just like the flickering of lights from the boat. And there was no more thunder, just like there was no more monster. Scarlett wished she could find the same peace after the storm as one feels in their bed once everything outside calms. But it was impossible. She would never feel peace again. Ever. She was that child terrified of the clown under her bed at night. She was the teenage girl trying to escape the man with knives as fingers as she ran out of a movie and into reality. There was nothing that would ever take this monster away. It would go on with Scarlett forever. Until she took her last breath, that monster would sit, sleep, eat, and bathe right next to her. Watching her. Breathing her in. Feeling her skin as she slept. Ivy would always be the hands under the dark water pulling at her feet, trying to pull her down to the bottom of the dark lake to be with her. Unlike this cliffside protecting them from the storm, nothing of this world could protect her from Ivy. Dead or alive. She would be with Scarlett. Always.

Chapter Fifty-Three

NOW

It took some convincing at the break of dawn, but the detective allowed Liam to board one of the rescue boats. After IV fluids, a clean change of clothes, and gym shoes from his truck, he was ready to return to the cove. The night was over, and the storm had passed; it was finally time to find answers.

The rain had changed the blue-green water to a brown, murky color. Logs from the flooded banks floated in the water, making their journey dangerous and tricky. But they didn't falter. A large tugboat was following close behind. It would pull Liam's sunken boat to the surface.

They turned the corner and finally reached the end of the cove. The rope was still hanging loosely from the tree. Navy blue cushions from the sofa floated on top of the water.

He imagined everything else from the boat now resting on the bottom of the lake.

Liam's eyes darted everywhere, begging the universe for anything that would tell him that his family was not down there. But he saw nothing until he looked over at the rocky bank. The rocks and mud had visible tracks coming from the water. "Take me over there!" Liam ordered.

Within seconds he was following the trail left behind by Scarlett and his children. He screamed their names into the forest as he stumbled and pushed briars and limbs out of the way. For the first time in a long time, he felt hope. The tracks went cold, but he kept moving. He kept looking, searching for any clue he could find. He listened for Kimber's cry, Ben's tiny voice, or Scarlett's precious one.

"Scarlett?!" He cried out, then waited for her to call back to him. But she didn't. They had to be out there somewhere. They just had to.

He almost missed it. He wouldn't have seen the small foot peeking out from a crevice between two rocks if he had not looked hard to the left. The fog was thick, but he was positive it was Ben's little foot.

Liam inched toward them slowly. Preparing himself for anything. He had no idea how long they had been out here like this. He had no idea if they were even together. He only saw one little foot.

His lungs paused as he crouched to look. He almost fell back. His knees went limp again. "Scarlett? Baby?" He whispered. Her skin color wasn't the same as Ben and Kimber's, who was clinging to her tattered shirt for dear life. Liam reached out to touch her face. She was cold. "Help!

Over here! We need help!" Liam shouted as the others caught up and could see what he was seeing.

"Come here, babies." Liam touched Ben and Kimber gently. Before they even opened their eyes, they started to scream and claw at Scarlett. Digging into her blue skin and burying their faces into the darkness of her body.

"Shhh, it's okay. It's Daddy. Come here. We have to help Scarlett. She's very sick." Kimber moved to his voice but kept her eyes closed. Her body was frail and weak. Ben's teeth were clenched, and his jaw was tight. His clothes were still damp. Liam hugged them tight, took the warm blankets from the rescue worker, and wrapped them together like a caterpillar in a cocoon. A flash of Ivy tucking them in their beds, saying, "Tight as a bug in a rug," as they giggled. But they aren't giggling today. The kids are in shock but will be okay in time. Liam would make sure of it. But he didn't know if he could save Scarlett.

When the kids moved away from her, her arms fell to her sides into the dirt and broken rocks. Her neck slumped forward, and her hair covered her face. "Scarlett, baby. It's Liam." His voice cracked. He wrapped his arms around her body and pulled her from the crevice between the boulders beneath the cliff. He laid her on the ground and let the rescue workers and first responders take over. A woman with her hair pulled tight in a low bun at the nape of her neck placed an oxygen mask over Scarlett's face while others took her vitals. Liam's lungs paused as he held his, but his heart ran wild. His hands shook as he waited. He watched as the paramedics assessed the children and then looked back to Scarlett. Everyone worked diligently to help her.

"I'm too late." Liam looked at the detective as he spoke into his radio, requesting an emergency medical helicopter transport.

Detective Karnes placed his hand on Liam's shoulder.

"She has a faint pulse, but her vitals aren't stable. We'll intubate and get her into the air to the hospital as soon as possible. Then we'll know more." The woman who spoke never looked in Liam's direction. She kept working to keep Scarlett alive.

"We need to get the kids back to the boat. There's an ambulance waiting for them at the dock." The rescue worker picked up Ben and followed a small crew back toward the lake. Liam looked back at Scarlett, then over at Kimber. He leaned toward Scarlett's face and whispered to her, "You're going to be okay. I'll be with you as soon as I can. I love you. Thank you. I'm sorry," tears rolled down his cheeks as he kissed Scarlett, maybe for the last time.

Then he scooped his smallest caterpillar into his arms, and they rushed back to the rescue boat in the cove as a group. He looked back only for a second at Scarlett, praying that he didn't lose her, even if he didn't deserve her.

He heard screaming ahead as they approached the cove. Liam immediately knew it was Ben and nearly fell as he stumbled over the rocks with Kimber in his arms. As he got closer, he saw that Ben was fighting with all he had not to get close to the water. He was kicking and punching one of the men in a blue rescue uniform.

"Ben, listen to me!" Liam handed Kimber to the detective. "It's okay, I promise. Stop. Ben, stop! Look at me." Ben stopped screaming and swinging his tiny fists at the sound of his father's voice. "This boat is going to get us out of here safely. You are safe. I'm right here. I promise."

Ben's rageful eyes changed to sadness. "Mommy's down there," his dirty, tiny finger pointed to the water. "Scarlett wouldn't help her. I was telling her, but she didn't help her." He was crying hard now, and Liam hugged him tight. His body was a few pounds lighter than it was just days ago.

"It's going to be okay, Ben." He assured him as they stepped into the boat. Ben's face buried into his father's shoulder like it was moments earlier when he was with Scarlett. Liam knew he had just lied to his son. It wasn't going to be okay. It was never going to be okay in his little world ever again. Whether Ivy was dead at the bottom of the lake or not, Ben no longer had a mother. She was gone.

Chapter Fifty-Four

NOW

"She needs more time," Dr. Edwards kept her voice low and stared intently into Liam's worried eyes as they sat in the chairs outside Scarlett's room on the intensive care floor.

"It's been a week." Liam looked away.

"As I said before, her brain needs rest. She suffered a huge amount of head trauma. Honestly, she's lucky to be alive. Just a few more days, and then we will start weaning her off the meds."

"And then we will know… you know, if she's going to wake up? If… she's going to be okay?" He cleared his throat. It had been seven very long days of not knowing. It was torturous.

"And then, we will know." She closed the chart, gave Liam a couple of comforting taps on his left shoulder, and rose to her feet.

"Thank you, Dr. Edwards." He didn't stand until the woman with long brown hair, a pointy nose, and a kind soul walked down the hall and then disappeared.

He always wondered if, by chance, he would find Scarlett sitting up and smiling at him when he opened the hospital room door. And every time, including this time, she wasn't.

The machine that breathed for her whispered to him from across the room, and his heart filled with disappointment. The smell of antiseptic and bandaids burned his nose, day after day. Everything was quiet. The television was off, and the phone didn't ring. The new cellphone Liam had bought for her and placed on her bedside table was unlocked and ready to call him if she should open her eyes.

Day after day, he was greeted with silence and disappointment. Everything was the same. The same IV pump to the left of her bed rested by the window with blinds closed. The same tubing and metal poles surrounded the head of her bed. A foley bag hung off the side of the hospital bed full of light-colored urine. Nothing changes.

Except one thing was different today. Liam immediately noticed the foreign object lying beside Scar's left arm in the bed. It lay near the nurse's call light button that Scarlett had never used as she had been in a coma since she arrived. Obviously, Liam didn't retain all the crime shows he watched on TV or the true crime podcasts Scar loved to listen to when they rode in the car. Because if he had, he wouldn't have touched it. He wouldn't have put it to his nose and closed his eyes. He wouldn't have read the note. He would have called the police instead.

But like most of the cases, he watched or listened to; he did what many family members or friends close to the victim often did, and he touched the evidence. He disturbed the crime scene and then destroyed it.

It wasn't until that night, after Liam had bathed the kids, put them safely to bed, locked all the doors, checked the windows, and set the security alarm, did he pull the object from his jacket pocket.

He read the two words scribbled on the get-well-soon card purchased from the hospital gift shop over and over. He knew, without a doubt, that only he would ever believe those two words were true. He also knew that all the people dragging the bottom of the lake could stop. They wouldn't find anyone down there.

Liam should have called Detective Karnes right away. After all, they speak every day while still searching for Ivy. But he didn't call him. He wasn't thinking. He panicked. He's embarrassed to admit that as soon as he saw what he saw lying near Scarlett's hand on the bed, he froze with fear and quickly looked behind him. He slowly turned the knob to look inside the small patient closet. Then he quickly flipped the old switch inside the small bathroom, his eyes open wide, ready for whatever awaited in the darkness. He even looked under the bed, terrified of what he might find. In his nightmares, that "what" is Ivy. He imagines dripping wet hair, black teeth, and broken, dirty fingernails from clawing her way out of the lake. Thankfully, no such thing was lying beneath Scarlett's hospital bed as she fought for her life.

Tonight, as Liam sat on the edge of the bed he used to share with his wife, that creature was everywhere. She hid in the shadows of the darkened room. She perched in the tree outside, watching him through the window. Perhaps she was lying still in the back seat of his truck, waiting for the next time he left the house.

He checked the locks one more time. He checked on the kids sleeping soundly in their beds one more time. Then he called the detective, who sounded tired and frustrated. He told him what he found, and Detective Karnes grew quiet. Silence stole the line. "I panicked; I'm sorry."

It wasn't until Liam ran his thumb over the wilting, pale pink rose petal that he realized the importance of this simple thing from Scarlett's room. It hadn't been his to take. But he took it anyway.

"What did the card say, Liam?"

Liam pulled it from his pocket. He had to straighten it out, as he had crumpled it in his sweaty palm earlier at the hospital, then shoved it inside his pocket alongside the one long stem pale pink rose.

It says, "*I'm sorry,*" Liam whispered, reading the note aloud for the detective. Liam felt afraid, sad, and guilty all at once.

"Don't do anything else, and don't go anywhere, I'll get forensics together, and we will be there in thirty minutes. Got it?"

"I got it." Liam tossed the crumpled card onto the kitchen counter beside the broken green stem as if it was something poisonous.

It didn't take thirty minutes for everyone to arrive, but it had felt like hours to Liam. The forensics team retrieved the items Liam had foolishly taken from Scarlett's hospital room, placed them in evidence bags, and left. The detective looked like his swollen, saggy eyes had collected a little more baggage over the past week. Joining the detective was a woman Liam had never met before.

"Liam, this is Dr. Trimble. She's a psychoanalyst we use for some of our more complex cases, like this one. Her expertise is quite useful. We've had great outcomes with her help."

"Hello, Dr. Trimble. It's nice to meet you." Liam offered his hand, and she took it, then covered it with both of her warm, soft hands. She looked at him with sympathy-filled eyes.

"Hello, Liam. Please call me Fern. I'm so sorry for everything you and your family are going through right now. I understand your girlfriend is in a coma and suffered an extensive head injury?" She didn't let go of Liam's hands and stood as close as a friend might.

"Yes, we hope she will wake up in a few days. The doctor says she needs to rest her brain just a while longer."

"And your children, how are they adjusting and processing everything that has happened?" The fifty-something woman with graying hair pulled tight into a knot on the top of her head had pale blue eyes and a kind face.

"Kimber isn't sleeping well at night or taking her naps. She refuses to eat. She asks for her mama all the time." Liam broke his hand away and wiped away a tear while clearing his throat. "And Ben, um, he is quiet. He's angry. He thinks his mom is dead. He has breakdowns over everything, even putting his shoes on."

"This must be a very difficult time for you, Liam. But these things will get better. People heal, and children are resilient. From what I've heard, you are a wonderful father, and I think you and your family will get through this."

Liam sat on the sofa and asked the detective and Fern to sit as well.

"Liam, when we searched the house last week after the incident in the cove, we found a journal. Ivy's journal. That's when we felt it would be best to call in Dr. Trimble for a little help."

"Help?" Liam felt confused and worried.

"Liam," Fern scooted toward the edge of the loveseat sitting on the other side of the coffee table, "basically, with everything we know about Ivy, it's clear that she's unwell and has been for quite some time. I've thoroughly examined her medical charts, all the evidence, and her journal so that I may better understand Ivy and her actions. I think it's obvious that the concern is with her mental health."

"She's not a psychopath if that's what you're trying to say. Ivy was fine until she had postpartum depression, and then..." his voice broke, and he hesitated, "then I had an affair," he continued, "She's been pushed to her limits, and she lost it for a little while, but she's not that. She's not a psycho." Liam stood and slammed the journal the detective handed him onto the wooden coffee table.

"Ivy is a third-grade teacher. She plays the piano at church on Sunday mornings and has friends who love her. She never goes to the grocery store without buying Holden his favorite rawhide. She plays hide and seek with Ben outside. She rocks Kimber every night and hums to her until she falls asleep." Liam tries his best not to sound as crazy as he feels right now. "And she was a wonderful, faithful wife to me. I realize that she's in trouble, as she should be. And I know that everything she has done recently is out of this world insane, but Ivy meant what she wrote on that card to Scarlett. She's sorry." All the hate he felt on the way to the lake the day they pulled Scarlett's car from the water has dissipated, and he blames himself.

"We all want Ivy to get better, Liam. We all want the same thing. No one is calling your ex-wife or the mother of your children crazy. But there are a few things that I'd like to talk to you about. I think she suffers from something worse than postpartum depression, an affair, or divorce." Fern put on her expensive, wired framed glasses, pulled a manilla file from her briefcase on the floor beside her, and started with the journal. "There were many entries where Ivy was obviously having a bad day or facing a difficult situation, and in those moments, she would begin interacting with a woman named Tia. And Tia was sort of this safe place for Ivy. She comforted her, she helped her be brave, and in ways, Tia was an alter ego of Ivy. Tia was mentioned here and there initially, but it was daily the past several months."

Detective Karnes then opened a file, "We questioned Ivy's close friend, Joseph. It had been mentioned that Ivy and Tia recently visited Ivy's old family cabin and had an accident. She stated that Tia called Joseph for help. Joseph stated that wasn't the case. He says that he never met Tia and that Ivy was alone on the day of her accident; it was she who called him asking for help. According to our investigation, there isn't any evidence of phone records, photos, texts, or emails from a woman named Tia. And I understand that you are aware that she somehow misconstrued your old girlfriend with her imaginary friend she calls Tia?"

Liam ran his hand through his messy hair that still needed a trim. "I don't know why she would lie about having a friend or knowing my ex-girlfriend from a long time ago."

"Ivy didn't intentionally lie. She believes Tia is real. We think she created her unconsciously to deal with things, as a child might do with an imaginary friend. I've seen where patients create these "friends" and give them the parts of themselves that are difficult to show or be. As I said earlier, Tia was brave; she was everything Ivy needed from herself to function."

"Patients? You said, *patients.* Are you referring to mentally ill patients?"

"Some patients with severe cases of Bipolar Disorder, Schizophrenia, or Psychosis. So, yes. People who experience hallucinations, hear voices, and try to balance normal sanity in front of family members or peers but find themselves in troubled situations, much like Ivy, can be diagnosed and treated. There were a couple of entries recently where Ivy disassociated herself and wrote from the perspective of Scarlett. It was pretty disturbing."

Liam's heart raced, and his hands grew sweaty as he imagined Ivy writing in the dark at night, alone with the kids, pretending to be his girlfriend. He felt like he was in a nightmare, and realistically, he was. They all were and had been for a while and didn't even know it. Unfortunately for

Liam and the kids, this nightmare isn't one you ever wake up from. Long after this mess is resolved, they will always need to protect themselves from a woman who was supposed to love them most in the world. Someone they do love most in the world. Now, Ivy would always be that *thing* waiting for them under their beds or watching them from the shadows in the corner of a darkened room. "I'm listening," his voice was low as we waited for the doctor to continue.

"She imagined Ivy sleeping at night, and Scarlett entered the home. She wanted to know things about Ivy. For instance, were there dishes in the sink, was the home tidy, what was Ivy really like. She was jealous, envious, curious, and resentful. Scarlett knew that you still loved Ivy and always would. She didn't like that, she didn't like Ivy, and she meant to do her harm. She described in her entry that Scarlett stole the boat keys from her purse. But we all know that isn't true, and Ivy lied to Joseph about this so that she would have access to the boat, and he wouldn't."

"So, if this wasn't a breakdown, what is wrong with Ivy?" Liam sat back down, facing the detective and doctor.

"I have no way of knowing what kind of diagnosis or prognosis we are dealing with without actually speaking with Ivy. If and when she is located, I promise to evaluate her extensively, and hopefully, with some treatment, she can be the mother she was before. A healthy one. With a lot of support, of course."

"And Liam, it's important to note if Scarlett doesn't wake up, whether they have to pull the plug or she dies naturally from all of this… Ivy will be charged with murder," The detective chimed in.

"I understand that, as she should," Liam replied defensively. Hate mixed with love for Ivy swirled in his boiling blood. How could he be angry with her if she's sick? He shouldn't, but he is.

"In the meantime, I've got an officer posted outside her hospital room. There's not going to be any more unseen visitors. We stopped searching the lake and have a warrant out for her arrest. I'll have your house and street manned at all times. If you find anything else, please, do not touch it. Call me instead. Immediately. Call me if you think she is nearby or she contacts you."

"Of course I will. Thank you, detective.

"One last thing, Liam, is Ivy's mother still alive?" Fern flipped through some paperwork.

"No, her mother died of Cancer. It was very traumatic for her. Ivy listened as her mother took her last breaths. She said she would never forget the sound." Liam answered.

The doctor's mouth gaped open with surprise; then she quickly offered Liam a small smile. "I'm looking forward to seeing you soon. Be patient with the kids. And take care of yourself. Talk to someone," Fern gathered her things and followed the detective to the front door.

"I will, thank you." Liam had been patient and taking care of himself, but the only person he wanted to talk to was lying in a hospital bed across town, fighting for her life. Liam wanted a drink, a strong one.

Chapter Fifty-Five

NOW

Liam's mom had come to stay and help with the kids. This was both helpful and burdening at the same time. It was like the hot, dry summers when you need it to rain, and then when it does, the air becomes humid, and debris collects in the lake, just waiting to take out a propeller or two. So yeah, this was like that in many ways. But Liam didn't trust babysitters or friends to keep the kids while he went to the hospital to be with Scarlett.

He would start back to work next week, still remote, thankfully. The kids would return to daycare until Ben started preschool in the fall. Life was moving on; even though Scarlett was still in a coma, Ivy was still missing, and Liam was still in shock most days. But time wasn't stopping; it wasn't even slowing down.

So, it was necessary to accept his mother's offer to assist. She had been kind and respectful of Liam's space and instructions for Ben and Kimber, but Liam hated the way she asked questions about the past, what was going on now, and what to expect for their future. She longed for answers he didn't have. He hated how the house was starting to smell like the home he grew up in instead of the home he and Ivy had shared. The things in the house belonged to Ivy, and how she cleaned and cared for the house were all touched and altered by his mother. He hated it. It is easier for the kids to stay at Ivy's. It's also closer to the hospital. Even Holden misses Ivy. He refuses to take the same kind of bones from Liam. That was always Ivy's thing, and Holden knew that.

Today is the day. The day Liam prays that Scar opens her eyes. The day she breathes all by herself. The day the rest of her can also start to heal with him. He missed her. In ways he never thought he would. She deserved so much better than him. He would offer her an out and ask if she wanted him to let her go. Parts of him believed she should say yes. Most of him hoped she would want to leave the hospital and come home to him and the kids. They were like a family before all of this, and he would give anything to be that again. It would be different now. Scar would be a full-time mom. And that was Ivy's fault. So, he couldn't feel guilty about that.

Liam tries to imagine if Ivy is found, treated, and sent back into the world to assume all the roles that belonged to her before everything she did, but he can't fathom it. He could never imagine Ivy rocking Kimber or helping Ben wash his hair in the bath. Liam was angry now. Things were becoming clearer. And even though Ivy couldn't help that she was sick, he had to hold her accountable. Liam learned that Ivy had been put on anti-psychotic medications after she was released from the hospital when she wrecked the car. She stopped taking them and stopped talking to her therapist, whom Liam never knew she was seeing in the first place.

"We have stopped the meds; now we wait. We'll closely monitor Scarlett's vitals and run more back-to-back tests to measure her brain activity." Dr. Edwards touched Liam's hand as he sat in the chair beside Scarlett, then left the hospital room.

The machines were no longer whispering. Only silence filled the room. Liam put her hand in his and moved a strand of hair from her face. "You're so beautiful, Scar. I probably didn't tell you that as often as I thought it. I should have told you more. But I thought it a million times a day when I looked at you. So, you would've probably hit me and told me to shut up if I told you over and over that many times in one day." He swiped away a tear and let out a small version of a laugh.

"I've been here every day, and I, um, well, I've never been able to talk to you," He cleared his throat as his voice started to crack. "I've not said everything that I've wanted to. But, um, I think maybe it's now or never. And I hope you'll hear my voice and come back to me. Back to us. Because we love you. Ben and Kimber love you, and I love you," He was crying now, his whispers so quiet that his heart beat louder than his voice. "You did so good. I'm so proud of you. You saved the kids' lives. And I know it wasn't easy. I know it must've been the hardest thing you've ever done. Thank you, baby. Thank you for all of it. And I'm so sorry. I'm sorry that I brought you into all of this. And I'm sorry that I didn't protect you better." He laid his forehead onto her hand and closed his eyes as he sobbed. "It's been a long time since you left that night. A long time since I've heard your voice. I miss you so much that I can't imagine living this life without you in it. I want to keep you forever. I want to give you everything, care for you, and love you as you deserve every day until I stop breathing. I'd give anything for you to open your eyes and come home with me and be with us. Start a new life. One far away from all of this bullshit. And if you don't choose to be with me. Then that's okay. I'll accept that. I'll understand if this has all been too much, and you need to move on. Just wake up. Breathe, Scar. Please!" Liam begged as he cried and squeezed her hand. But she just slept, and everything was still quiet. She didn't open her eyes, speak to him, or even take a deep breath. She lay there in the deepest sleep. Such a deep sleep, Liam worried she might never wake up.

Chapter Fifty-Six

NOW

"Make sure to brush your teeth for Grandma and say your prayers before bed. Daddy will be home soon, I promise." Liam told Ben over the phone. He didn't tell him Scarlett wasn't waking up, and her brain was still sleeping.

Liam stayed long after his promise. Never turning on the television to watch the baseball game. Never checking his phone for messages or emails. He just sat with her in silence until Dr. Edwards entered the dark hospital room.

"It's time for another EEG. You should go home and get some rest. I promise we will call you if anything changes."

Liam debated, then checked his watch. It was nearly 2 am. He needed to go home and walk Holden. His mother had been a huge help with the kids, but she didn't have the strength to walk a full-grown golden retriever. Besides, Liam didn't want her outside after dark, alone. It was a house rule. It wasn't safe. Not yet. Maybe not ever.

"I love you. I'll be back. First thing in the morning. I promise," Liam kissed Scarlett's clammy skin.

"Thank you, Dr. Edwards."

"Of course, Liam," She held the door for him to step out into the hall and allow the radiology team to come inside and transport Scarlett upstairs for her test.

The ride home was lonely. He had grown used to it but hoped this night would be different. He had hoped that Scarlett would be awake and he would be able to breathe deeper. He had been holding his breath for so long now he wasn't sure he could ever breathe normally again.

He slept three hours. That was enough. He was parking his truck in the hospital parking garage by 6:45 am. He hadn't waited for Ben to jump on him in bed or hear Kimber calling out to him in her baby bed over the monitor on his nightstand. He showered and left. Something inside of him told him to. And it's Sunday. Sundays are still Sundays. They chase him down and eat him alive every week. But what he wouldn't give for everything to be like it was months ago. He wished Ivy was sitting at the piano with the kids at church. Although, he wouldn't be spending his time running and stealing a few moments to sit outside by that tall tree and listen to his ex-wife's music. He'd be somewhere else, anywhere else…with Scarlett. Starting a new day. A whole new life. Like it was a Monday. And he wished that Ivy wasn't sick. That she was well and not her own worst enemy. But, unfortunately, this was just a normal Sunday. There were no shooting stars in the sky to wish on, no genies in a bottle to rub. No wishes were being granted today.

Liam walked through the parking garage, then up the stairs to the skyway to the hospital, where he took the elevator to the neuro intensive care unit on the fourth floor. He walked past the nurse's desk, which was starting to come alive as the patients were waking and needing things like their medicines and help going to the bathroom. But Scar's hospital room door, with the number *407* on it, was still closed. And he imagined her lying inside like a forgotten promise. He knows that the doctors and nurses care for her well, but she's always alone if he's not there. And he hates the thought of that.

He grabbed onto the cold door handle and hesitated. What if he opened the door, and finally, after all this time, she was awake? His heart skipped a beat as he prayed harder than usual, turning the handle and pushing the door open. But then all hope was lost. A lump formed in his throat. He couldn't speak. Liam looked down the hall at the nurse's station, but everyone was too busy to notice him as he panicked. No officers were posted outside the hospital room to monitor everyone coming and going. The room he had been coming to for so long felt foreign and unfamiliar. He looked at the bed and then back at the nurse's station, confused and scared. The bed was empty. Not empty like she had been taken somewhere for tests, but empty like she was gone and not coming back. The bed was made properly with fresh sheets. The blinds were open, and the sunshine filled the room. All the IV pumps and poles were gone. No machines were whispering and then waiting to be needed again. The room had always been quiet, but now you could hear a pin drop. Liam even checked the numbers on the door again. Yeah, he was in the right room.

"Liam."

He heard his name and jumped. When he turned to see Dr. Edwards standing in the doorway, he was relieved and terrified at the same time.

"Dr. Edwards? Where's Scarlett."

"I thought you might already be here. Sit down for a minute. Let's talk."

Dr. Edwards entered the room and moved closer to Liam as he stepped backward.

"I don't want to sit. Where's Scarlett?"

The doctor paused, and Liam noticed she was holding a clear plastic ziplock bag. He could see the iPhone he had left Scarlett for when she woke up; he knew hers was lost. He could also see the photo he had left for her as well. He could see two smiling faces looking back at him. It felt like the day they took that picture was an eternity ago, maybe even a different life altogether.

"No." Liam shook his head back and forth, then shoved his hands in his jeans pockets while stepping backward until he reached the hospital bed. Then he sat; he had no choice; the empty room was spinning, and feared he might not have the strength to stand on his own two feet much longer. Then he listened as his heart broke into a million pieces.

Chapter Fifty-Seven

NOW

"She's all yours." Liam dropped the keys into the new homeowner's hand and watched her smile grow wide.

"Thank you!"The young newlyweds shook Liam's hand; then they were up the sidewalk and inside the house before he could blink.

It started snowing, and the cold breeze made Liam's bones shiver. "Let's go, boy," he opened his truck door, and the obedient golden retriever hopped in and made himself comfortable in the front passenger seat next to Liam.

As the truck drove down the street away from the home he and Ivy had created and destroyed their family in, he didn't look back. He couldn't.

The new year had come and gone. Liam had been packing the moving trailer as he listened to people in their homes celebrating. He did that a lot. Watched and listened as others went on with their lives like normal while he was stuck in this place. Not really a place, but a state of mind. Even Ben was back to running his little diecast metal tractors through the snow playing again. Kimber was sleeping through the night in her own bed and laughing at funny things again. Life was coming together. No one had seen even a trace of Ivy. No more single roses or notes had been left. It was as if the world swallowed her whole. So Liam sold the house, then packed everything he wanted to keep and donated everything he didn't. It was the most therapeutic thing he could do but also one of the hardest. It's all that's left of Ivy and all that the kids will ever have of her. A part of Liam wanted to burn it down. But he wrapped her things in bubble wrap and packed them into storage containers. He didn't write her name or label those particular containers; he couldn't. So, he color-coded everything without even realizing it.

Her jewelry box, family photos, childhood memorabilia, favorite coffee mug, and clear heavy crystal vase Liam had bought her, the only vase he found in the house, as she must have thrown them all away, were packed. Five black containers were all Ivy had to show for her time here on this earth. That and her two precious children she nearly killed. Liam thought of the crystal vase. When he had returned home from the cove that day the boat was recovered, and the kids were found, the vase was on the dining room table. In it were dead long-stem roses. It's funny how Ivy told the truth about some things and lied about others. He guessed she could no longer distinguish the two by the time those roses had wilted.

Days later, Liam had the keys to their new home in his hand. The listing online boasted of a one-of-a-kind home nestled within the trees of a down-to-earth community surrounded by lakes and trails, offering the comfort of being away from the city. The pictures didn't do justice to the stunning entryway, Brazilian cherry wood finished floors with accented crown molding. So many windows provided natural light from both the sun and moon. A gourmet kitchen featuring custom cabinetry, professional grade appliances, and a charming open concept for entertaining. The house was nearly 5000 square feet and was everything to a tee that Scarlett had told Liam she wanted one day. He took one look at the house in person the last time he flew out with the kids to visit his mother and accept a new job; and knew this was the one. When the realtor asked if he'd like to look at other homes closer to his mother in the area, he declined. Nope, this one is it, he had said. And move-in day finally arrived.

Within a month, Ben's room was painted royal blue, bookshelves were built, and his new big boy bed was all set up. Kimber's pale pink room had a new round braided rug to play on next to her wooden toy box filled with her favorite dolls, blocks, and stuffed animals.

Their routine had been set, and Liam loved his new job. Finally, the hands on the clock were keeping time again. He was in the moment. He focused on being a father and a provider again. Everything else only got small pieces of him now and then.

The oven timer sounded, indicating the lasagna was done. Ben sat at the dinner table, drawing a picture for his favorite new teacher at school. Kimber was in her highchair nibbling on a pre-dinner piece of garlic bread. Just as the doorbell rang, Liam searched everywhere for that red oven mitt. The only one he owned. The timer was sounding again. "Yeah, yeah, I know. I'm trying," He looked in the drawer near the stove, pushing the aluminum foil and wax paper around, but no red oven mitt was there. The doorbell rang again. He's not sure why his mother always rings the doorbell, she knows the code to get in, but she insists, and most days, Liam appreciates it. Giving up, he used a large dish towel to remove the heavy glass casserole dish from the oven. The smell of lasagna was mesmerizing.

"Oh, kiddos, your dad just made the best-looking lasagna in the whole wide world." Kimber must have thought he was funny because she laughed out loud at him and then took another bite of her garlic bread.

"I'm coming!" Liam turned off the oven and headed toward the front door. As he left the kitchen, he noticed the red oven mitt next to two small toy tractors and a pile of Legos in the kitchen corner. "Well, that mystery is solved," Liam said to himself as he made his way to answer the door.

When Liam opened the door, no one was there. It was dark outside, and he was almost too late to notice the woman walking down the sidewalk toward her car in the driveway. He blinked and then blinked again while trying to find his voice to call out to her. But he just ran; he ran to her. "Wait! Please, wait!" He called out. That dish towel was still in his hand.

It was her. His heart sank. He couldn't see her clearly, but he was sure it was her. For a second, he was right back in that empty hospital room, listening to Dr. Edwards tell him that Scarlett had woken up, that she was doing well, that her brain function was unremarkable, and that she didn't want to see him ever again. She had been moved to another floor, and the authorities were with her taking her statement as we spoke. She also said that Scarlett would have a long road to recovery. Both physically and emotionally. Liam didn't protest. He took the clear plastic bag with the phone and photo, then left, just as Scarlett had wished. So at least someone's wish came true that day.

And now she was standing in the driveway of his new home in Colorado. "Scarlett, please. Stop." He watched her pause. "The kids are inside alone, and I can't stay out here long." He watched Scarlett wipe away a tear as she stood in the shadows near her opened car door. He didn't know what else to say. The snow was falling, clouding his view of the woman he still loved with his whole heart. "When I decided to move the kids out here to Colorado to be closer to my mom and have a fresh start, I found this house. I only looked at it once. It was similar to the house we discussed building one day." Liam looked back at the front door. He needed to go back inside to the kids. He heard the car door shut. Then Scarlett was walking toward him, stopping four feet away from him. Her hands were in her coat pockets, her shoulders straight, and beautiful long strawberry blonde curls fell down her arms. He wished she was close enough to see those freckles across her nose. She hated them, but Liam loved them.

"I just wanted to come see if you and the kids are okay. Are you? Okay, I mean?" Her voice was strained; she was trying not to cry.

"We are okay. Are you okay?" He tried to study her face, but she kept looking down and wiping at her cheeks.

"I'm better."

Liam drowned in the silence.

"I miss you." She whispered, yet he heard her loud and clear. It was everything he needed to hear her say. Just three words. He started to speak, but she ran into his arms. His skin was ice cold now, but he didn't care. He lingered with her in his arms for a moment, wondering if she was real and really in his arms like he had dreamt a million times.

"Liam, I'm sorry. You're freezing. You should go back inside and get warm."

"Come with me." The request was both simple and complex at the same time. They both knew she would be coming home forever if she walked through that front door. "If you want. I'd love for you to be here with us. With me."

She kissed him. She kissed him like that first night in his office. She kissed him like the night he asked her to stay forever. She kissed him like that day on the boat beneath the hot summer sun.

Then she took his hand, walked with him into the house, and closed the door behind them. Leaving both the cold and past outside.

Chapter Fifty-Eight

NOW

Liam believes that there are moments in life that are so monumental that pieces of our soul remain there in that moment in time forever. After that monumental moment, we are never the same. Hopefully, we are better, we've learned, and we've grown, but ultimately we recall on that moment when we need to. We see the world from the perspective of that piece of us that didn't move forward in life with us. Liam has left behind many pieces of himself throughout time. He no longer takes life for granted. He also doesn't trust as easily and always looks with his eyes wide open, literally and figuratively.

As the months passed, he could tell that a large part of Scar remained in that cove back at the lake. Her eyes are different. They're still full of love and life but are now skeptical, and sometimes as wide as Liam's, both searching the faces of the people near them and the kids. They are always looking for Ivy, and they always would.

Liam had taken Ben to preschool and dropped Kimber off at daycare. It would be a day completely dedicated solely to Liam and Scarlett. No work, no kids, just a perfect day. He returned home to pick up Scarlett.

He called out to her once he got home, then locked the door behind him. After he removed his running shoes, he rushed through the living room only to step on a pine cone with his bare feet. "Damn it!" He quickly sat on the piano bench to check out his foot. Sure enough, it was a pine cone. Ben was obsessed with them; he had begun collecting them and bringing them inside, leaving them all over the house. It was starting to drive Liam nuts. But he picked his battles these days. Ben had come a long way. He understood that his mom was sick and that she was gone. Not because Scarlett left her in the water that night. She didn't sink, and she's not in the lake. Hopefully, she's somewhere safe and getting help. Liam tries not to encourage any hope or thoughts that she will ever be with them again because she won't be.

Liam realized he was sitting on the piano bench for the first time. It was the only piece of furniture that came with the house. He kept it only because it was so heavy, and Ben loves to play it. But he hates it. He loathes it. Sometimes when Ben plays at night, he imagines Ivy sitting at the piano in church teaching Ben to play. She threw all that away, and now Ben has suffered so much loss because of her carelessness. Liam slammed the piano shut and threw the pine cone into the kitchen trash can, again calling out Scarlett's name. As Liam made it through the house and up the stairs to their bedroom, he noticed pine needles all over the hardwood floor. That, too, had become a thing with Ben; he refuses to remove his shoes in the house and tracks in dirt everywhere. He even wants to sleep in them. Liam was concerned with the behavior, but the therapist said to go with it and pick his battles. So Liam overlooked the pine cones placed all over the house and the pine needles on the floor. He cleaned them up and hoped that eventually, Ben would stop.

Liam touched the bedroom doorknob and recalled the handle on the hospital door to Scarlett's room. He remembered how he felt every time he opened the door and hoped that she would be awake. He hesitated before opening the door. He feared that somehow Scarlett had slipped back into that deep sleep, where even his kiss couldn't wake her.

Once he went inside, she was, in fact, asleep, but his kiss did wake her. "Hey there, sleepy head." He whispered as he sat on the bed next to her.

"Hey." She smiled before she opened her sleepy eyes to look at him.

"You were supposed to be ready when I got back." He kissed her forehead. "I have the entire day planned out for us. All things you love. Hot mocha cappuccinos, omelets, then something fun, then something expensive, then something romantic, and then back to food. So you better get up if you don't want to miss out." He teased, kissing her lips.

"I vote we stay here. All day. Until time to pick up the kids."

"If we do that, we will end up doing stuff around the house, and then we will have to cook and clean up the kitchen and.." She interrupts him.

"Nope. We will stay here… in bed. Just like this." She pulls him close, kissing him back this time.

"I think I love your idea more than mine." He whispered while tasting her mouth.

Liam had fallen in love with watching Scarlett become the woman of the house. She was a natural with the kids. He loves watching her teach Ben how to crack an egg, and they laugh when he makes a mess. He loves watching her paint Kimber's toenails as she paints her own. But he loves this most. Being with Scarlett, just like this. In their home, in their bed. Nothing else matters. Not anything that happened last year. Not anything that could happen tomorrow.

But something is missing and will always be missing if Liam doesn't find it. It was what the whole day was supposed to be about. It was the romantic and expensive part he mentioned before they made love. Liam intended to do everything in his power right. And this would be the official beginning of a whole new life.

"Join me out by the firepit? I'll get it started, and then I'll bring out some breakfast?" Liam had started to drift off but was too determined to sleep.

"You are spoiling me, Mr. Cameron."

"You deserve the world, baby."

"Liam, I want you to know that I see you. I see everything you do to make things better and help us all heal. I feel all the things you feel inside." She touched the skin over his heart. "I appreciate every little thing you do. Being here with you and the kids, in this house you bought for us a million miles away from all the bad that happened last year, is everything

I want. I love you. Right here with you is where I belong. I love you, Liam."

His hand touched her cheek, and for a second, he wondered how many times he had imagined Scarlett in his arms saying these exact words. Millions he bet. He kissed her lips like the snowy night she came home to him.

"I love you too, Scarlett."

"Okay, I'm ready to wrap myself in this warm blanket and sit by the fire while you make a mess in the kitchen we will have to clean up later, just as you predicted earlier. Then we will meet back here for round two." She teased as she got out of bed and draped the soft blanket around her perfect naked body.

Liam wasn't nervous. In fact, he couldn't flip the egg on the gas stove fast enough. He would've made it out to the firepit in the backyard quicker had he not stepped on yet another pine cone on the kitchen floor, causing him to drop the cooked egg on the floor.

He growled as he cooked a whole new egg, ham, and cheese omelet. He had used all the peppers on the omelet he had to throw in the trash. Before he knew it, he served Scarlett breakfast and a mimosa out by the warm fire. They ate and laughed as they discussed all the phrases Kimber had learned and was saying now. Both were amazed at how much both kids had grown and changed since last summer.

The champagne glasses were empty, and the fire was warm. Liam held Scarlett as she sat in his lap, sharing the blanket. Scar was still naked, but he was not. They rested in silence, holding on to a moment they thought they might never have not so long ago.

"Scar?" Liam whispered.

"Hmmm?" Scarlett answered as her head lay on his chest.

"Will you marry me?" He asked.

Her head popped up off his chest, and she searched his dark eyes, verifying this moment was this perfect and real at the same time. A hint of a smile had already spread across her face.

"I've known for longer than I realized you are the one. I want this. You and me, just like this. Every day for the rest of our lives. I want you to be everything you are to Ben and Kimber forever. And one day, maybe we could try." He couldn't finish, but she followed his gaze to her abdomen. "A little bit of you and me running around. And then we can grow old and gray, and you can push my wheelchair around." Liam teased, and she laughed.

She watched as he pulled a small jewelry box from beneath the airodock chair they sat in together. "Scarlett, will you be my wife?" He opened the box.

Scarlett covered her mouth with one hand and held the blanket over her chest with the other. She looked at Liam and then at the gorgeous round diamond resting on a gold band. "Yes, Liam. I will marry you." She smiled as big as she had in the bedroom earlier that morning while making love to the only man she had ever loved.

Chapter Fifty-Nine

NOW

It was going to be an intimate, quaint ceremony, and it was going to be perfect. They only needed a couple of months to plan the wedding. Scarlett loved choosing every little detail, and Liam loved watching her do it. Somedays, it felt like he had never even walked down the aisle before, and then others, memories hung heavy over him like a large dark cloud. Most days, it all felt brand new. And in ways, this new life in this new place meant this was all brand new.

Forrest green and cream were their wedding colors. Both Liam and Scarlett had designed an archway made of tree limbs and bark, built custom, and delivered. It rested on the back lawn for now, but once the wedding was over, the arch's permanent home would be in a garden out back that they had decided to plant soon.

The chairs were stacked on the back porch near the firepit. Once the tent arrives the day before the wedding, which would be in six days, the reception tables and chairs would be set up, as well as a small dance floor and place for the band Liam and Scar had discovered one date night as they danced at a place in town.

Scarlett went on and on about the music, their dance, and their vows. But Liam wanted to hurry and get to when they finally say *I do.* He just wanted her to be his. Forever. In a sacred way, always. This time, he would know better, and all the mistakes he had made before wouldn't happen again. He'd look out for Scarlett in ways he didn't with Ivy. He had failed Ivy in the biggest of ways. He could never change any of it, and he couldn't make it better. It was just a failure he would have to always own. Yes, Ivy was sick, but wasn't it in his vows to honor her in sickness and health? When he mentioned this to his mom recently, she brushed it off and said he was only human. He had coped and did what most would have that weekend Ivy had told him she wanted him to leave. He found comfort out of desperation. He appreciated his mother's encouragement and support. He never regrets coming to live near her. They enjoyed Sunday family dinners, game nights, and spending time together as his family moved forward.

Liam closed his laptop, sitting on his home office desk. Excited that work was finished for a few days and happy that his vows were written and ready to say to Scarlett at the altar in less than a week. His day had been productive. His favorite part of his vows was the rawest and truest part. The part where he tells Scarlett that she saved him from Sundays.

It wouldn't be a normal walk through the house if Liam didn't dodge a million pine cones as he made his way to the bedroom. It was late. The kids had been in their beds fast asleep for hours. The last he saw of Scarlett, she was finalizing their honeymoon plans. They were booked for an Alaskan cruise. The kids were excited, and so was his mom. Taking your family and mother along on the honeymoon wasn't ideal, but both Liam and Scar didn't feel comfortable leaving the kids yet. And Liam promised her lots of alone time.

The cool sheets welcomed him as he quietly climbed into bed with Scarlett. The gas fireplace created shadows around the room. Liam pulled Scar close and nearly fell asleep when Ben came to their room like he does most nights.

He was sleepwalking and speaking gibberish. "Hey, buddy. Let's get you back to bed. More gibberish. This started a couple of weeks ago. Ben never remembered doing it the next day. The therapist said it was normal and would resolve itself soon to ensure the environment was safe and he didn't fall down the stairs or wander outside. Both were very scary things that terrified the hell out of Liam.

He picked up the little boy and carried him back toward his room. "Mama said to hurry," Ben mumbled as his head rested on his dad's shoulder. "You have to help Mama." He continued while still dreaming.

"It's okay, Ben. Everything's okay." *Damn you, Ivy, for putting our kids through everything you did.* Liam thought as he opened Ben's bedroom door, stepping on a hundred pine needles on the floor from the pine trees out back. He pulled the covers close to Ben's chin and tucked him in. It was then, when he turned to leave the room, that he noticed something crouching down in the corner near the window. The window was barely open, Liam could feel the spring breeze sneaking in and swarming around his bare feet. He froze, and chills went up his spine.

"Liam." Her whispers were familiar and unfamiliar at the same time. He didn't move.

A covered moan came from the corner. She sounded like an animal. Liam didn't know if he should run to call 9-1-1, grab Ben from his bed and run like hell, or scream for Scarlett, who could never hear him from Ben's bedroom on the first floor. He didn't know what to do, so he did nothing.

"Liam, please, help me." The voice was strained and in pain.

The creature in the shadows was jerking and moving uncontrollably. "Ivy, what are you doing here? What's wrong? Are you hurt?" He needed all those answers. Immediately.

But all he got was cries and panting. He moved closer, so he could see her better. He dreaded seeing her black decayed teeth, broken nails, and dirty skin. All the characteristics of the creature who hid under the bed after dragging herself out of the lake.

But as he moved closer, he saw that she was none of those things. Her long dark hair wasn't wet and tangled with debris from the bottom of the muddy water of that cove back in North Carolina. It was long, silky, and clean. Her hands were the same hands he used to hold. Her face was just as it was the night he asked her to dance for the first time. Immediately he knew it was easier to imagine Ivy as a monster than this. The monster he hates, but the Ivy he married long ago was the love of his life once upon a time.

"Ivy, what's wrong?" He whispered as he looked her over. It didn't take long for him to realize exactly what was causing Ivy so much pain. It was obvious from the size of her belly that she was pregnant. Without even thinking his hands were on her. Her skin was sweaty, and her stomach muscles were hard; she was in labor. She grabbed one of his hands and bit down on her lower lip as she squeezed her eyes shut and endured the contraction. Once it was over, her grip on his hand relaxed, and she laid back to rest. "I can't do this here. Come with me." She stood with his help, and he followed her out the front door. Liam noticed she knew the house's layout well.

As they rounded the corner of the house, Ivy stopped, cried out a muffled scream, and squatted. Liam stayed close. His heart was pounding. His knees grew weak as he watched her bear down hard. "We have to get you to a hospital, Ivy. Now!"

Her head shook back and forth quickly. "No!" She raised to her feet once again. She was wearing black leggings and an oversized navy blue sweater. She smelled the same way tonight that she did all the nights he had spent with he before she became a monster. She smelled like strawberries and champagne. It wasn't fair. It wasn't fair that she showed up here, and the universe stole all the hate and distaste he had for her and replaced it with all the feelings he felt before last summer. It wasn't fair, and he wouldn't forget everything that happened. He was never going to let go of Scarlett again. Not for a minute.

Ivy stood, took a deep breath, grabbed his hand again, and took off toward the backyard. As they ran through the grass that would be the aisle that Scarlett would walk down to him at the altar, Liam had a flashback of the last time he and Ivy had held hands and ran down the aisle to get out of the rain. It was just like this on their wedding day all those days ago. The rain grew heavy as Liam let her lead him past the pines and into the forest.

He could tell her legs were trembling as clear fluid leaked from her, staining her leggings. They went maybe twenty feet into the forest before she finally stopped and lay down. The branches mostly shielded them from the large raindrops, but they were still getting wet. Ivy didn't let go of his hand. She was panting and moaning while lying on her back.

"This is insane, Ivy! We have to get you help! I can't help you!" Liam went to stand, and she grabbed him, pulling him closer. Their noses were so close that their skin was nearly touching.

"You have to do this, Liam. You have to help us. Please." Then she squeezed her eyes and screamed out. This time she didn't hold back. She screamed so loud that the sound bounced off the canyons in the distance, and wolves howled back. Suddenly, they were no longer lying on the forest floor; they were at the hospital back in North Carolina. Ivy was giving birth to their child, and Liam was with her, just like this. She was his everything; he couldn't wait to hold their son. It's strange how some memories imprint on our souls forever, and others we forget in an instant.

"Please, Liam. Please." She whispered. She brought his hand to her mouth and softly kissed his skin. More flashes. Flashes of laughter bolted across his eyes like lightning. Flashes of her in his arms, happy and free of everything.

"Okay." Liam let the tears fall without care as he moved away and started to remove her leggings. She was barefoot. He inched the fabric down and off of her. She spread her legs apart, and Liam could see a head crowning in the moonlight, just like he had watched when she birthed Ben and Kimber.

Ivy was moaning and sweating even though it was a cold April night. Liam was only wearing pajama pants and a crew neck sweatshirt.

"Breathe, Ivy. Steady your breathing. Remember how we practiced in those birthing classes when you were pregnant with Ben?"

Ivy tried to do as he said. She tried hard. Lightning flashed, and thunder crashed down around them. It was loud, and Liam would have sworn that the ground shook.

She cried out, and Liam went to hold her. She was still trembling. He pulled the sweatshirt over his head and covered her. "It's okay; you're doing great." He said it over and over as she rested between contractions and pushing.

"I've missed you so much. I thought of a million ways to end my life, but when I realized I was pregnant, I couldn't do it. I've been lost for nine months. Missing you. Regretting everything I did." She started to cry from a different pain than the intense labor.

Liam didn't say anything. All the anger and fear trapped inside his soul, festering and growing, started to dissipate. All at once, it emerged from his guts and left him. Ivy wasn't a monster wishing to hurt them, she wasn't a criminal who calculated a plan and wanted their children to drown, and she wasn't some distraught crazy woman living in the woods, haunting them from afar. Or was she? Liam looked around at all the things from the house surrounding them. Wrappers from the whole grain bars in the pantry, empty water bottles were scattered all over, and a sleeping bag and pillow rested neatly near a large tree.

"I can see Ben's room from here. He lets me in, and I visit sometimes. We snuggle, and I tell him bedtime stories. But don't worry. I convinced him I wasn't real and it was all a dream. He leaves his window unlocked so I can shower and wash my clothes. Sometimes when I get tired from sleeping out here in the cold, I sleep in your bed during the day while everyone is gone. I remember what it was like to be the woman lying there next to you. I was happy when it was me with you and not her. I was so happy until I wasn't. I did my best, Liam. I missed a couple of doctor appointments, and then I ran out of refills, and it was going to take forever to get back in to see my therapist, so I just tried to go without my meds. And before I knew it, I didn't know what was real anymore. But don't worry; I'll go as soon as I have the baby. I'll take the baby and go. I'll miss the kids. I'll miss bringing Ben pine cones for him to play with. And sometimes, I pet Kimber's hair as she sleeps and realize I never get to see my children's faces in the sunlight, and I wonder what it would be like to take them with me. Away from you and away from her." Ivy pauses and bears down, crying out into the darkness. The rain slowed for now. His whole body grew tense as he listened to Ivy. I watch Scarlett with them. It's easy to see they love her. And I watch you with her too. And I know you love her like you loved me. So, I'll go. I'll leave you to marry her." A tear slid down her cheek, and she quickly wiped it away. Appearing ashamed and a little angry.

She looked into Liam's eyes, and his heart broke for her all over again. She wasn't well. As soon as she delivered the baby, he would call an ambulance. She needed help. She couldn't live in the forest with a baby. She couldn't take care of herself, let alone a newborn.

She screamed out louder this time. Liam went to look. "Ivy, it's time. It's time for one good push. The baby's head is almost out. Push Ivy! Push!"

"I can't! I'm splitting in two! God help me!" Ivy leaned on her elbows, letting her head fall back as she screamed in pain.

"You can do this, Ivy. Just like before, just like with Ben and Kimber. The baby needs you to push. Push Ivy!" Ben held her trembling legs as she pushed as hard as she could.

And just like that, the baby was out. Liam could see even in the darkness that its color was more blue than pink. He remembered the color of Scareltt's skin the day he found her with the kids near the lake, and he felt vomit rise into his throat, burning his entire chest.

He rubbed the baby's chest vigorously with the palm of his hand. "Breathe, sweetie, breathe. Come on!" The baby let out a weak cry and tried opening its eyes.

"Thank God," Ivy said as she fell back off her elbows and onto the pine needles. Liam noticed a picture frame on the ground nearby. It was of the four of them at the beach when Kimber was just a small infant. Liam slammed the frame down hard onto a tree root sticking up from the cold ground, shattering the glass. He then used a shard of glass to cut the cord. He had done it twice before, so he knew where to go. He then picked a weed and tied it around the remaining cord attached to the baby. Seconds later, Ivy's knees were bent, and she cried out as the placenta expelled onto the forest floor she had been sleeping on for God know's how long.

"It's a boy. We have another son, Ivy."

"Can I hold him?" Liam hesitated and then looked at the mother with her arms held out, and he reached her the baby. And just like human nature works, the baby was at Ivy's breast, and she was covering it with Liam's sweatshirt. The crying stopped.

"You did so good, Ivy."

She smiled at him with tears streaking down her face. "We did good. Thank you." She squeezed his hand, and he squeezed back, letting his tears mix with the rain.

"Ivy, we need to get help. The baby needs to see a doctor. I can carry you both back to my truck."

"No! I told you I would go. I'll take our son and go. You don't have to worry about us. I'll never come back. I just needed to come back to you for this. I couldn't do this part without you."

Liam wanted to lash out at the universe. Damn it. Why was Ivy like this? Why?! He wanted the old Ivy back. He needed her for the kids, for their new baby… for him.

Suddenly he was sitting on the couch at their house in North Carolina. Dr. Fern Trimble was sitting on the loveseat with Detective Karnes across from Liam. She used words like psychosis, schizophrenia, Bipolar disorder, severe, patient, and treatment when referring to his ex-wife. All that fear and torment from before returned. It was like someone pressed play on an old VCR, and a horror movie began. The woman holding their child was like a shapeshifter; she was his ex-wife and the kid's mother one second, and the next, she was all the terms Dr. Trimble used that night.

He had to convince Ivy to come with him. "Ivy, we can make this work. We can be together. We just have to make sure you and the baby are okay. I don't know what I'm doing."

She looked at him with familiar kind eyes. Soft eyes. Sad eyes. His wife's eyes. "I love you, Liam. From that first moment in Charlotte, I loved you." She swallowed hard as the baby nursed, and her abdomen contracted. I never meant to hurt you or the kids. Or Scarlett." She started to cry.

"It's okay, baby. I'm here. Everything is going to be okay. Just come with me. Please." She allowed him to help her sit up. She looked down at the baby she had just given birth to. "He has your nose." She whispered.

Liam looked at the little boy in her arms. She was right; he did. "Look at all that hair. Just like Kimber when she was born. Remember?"

"Yeah, she did have a lot of hair." Ivy petted the baby's scalp softly. "What should we name him?" Ivy looked into Liam's eyes, and he couldn't help but to move a strand of hair from her face and touch her cheek.

"You can name him whatever you like," Liam answered.

"Barrett. I think he looks like a *Barrett*." She replied, lightly touching the baby's skin as the love of her life was still touching hers.

"It's perfect, Ivy."

"I'll go, but you can't leave me. You have to stay with me. Promise?" Ivy asked with her entire being. "Promise me, Liam."

"I promise." He removed his hand from her cheek and started helping her up so he could carry her back to the house and call for help. But a limb on the ground snapped behind them.

"Liam? Oh my God! What's going on, Liam?!" Scarlett was covering her mouth, trying not to scream in fear.

And just like that, Ivy's body tightened. She retreated like a frightened animal, scurrying on the ground with the baby still clutched onto her breast.

"Scarlett, listen to me; everything is okay. Go home." He had both hands on her shoulders, begging her. He knew Ivy would never do what he asked now that Scarlett was present.

"What's happening? You're covered in blood!"

Liam looked down at his hands, arms, and chest. She was right; Ivy's blood was all over him. The baby cried out.

"Is that a baby?" Her eyes grew wide, her hands covered her mouth, and she started to tremble.

"Go! Please, Scarlett. Go home now!" He demanded. He had never screamed at her like that before. Never.

She took steps backward toward the house Liam had bought for her. The house they had spent the past couple of months building a home in. But all those safety walls were caving in all around them.

Liam knew the ground wasn't shaking, and the world wasn't ending, but it sure felt like it.

"Ivy, come here. It's okay. She's gone. Everything is okay." He found her propped up against a pine tree.

He moved closer, and she let him. She was weak and bleeding a lot. He had to get her to a hospital. Fast.

"Liam?" Her voice sounded as weak as she looked. "Do you love her?"

Her question made his insides quiver, and she could tell. A tear rolled down her cheek. "Let me ask that question better. Do you love her more than me?" She was pitiful. And Liam didn't know what to say.

His love for her and his love for Scarlett were two very different things. It couldn't be compared or be measured against the other. It wasn't equal, just different.

Her eyes searched into his intently, and she knew. He knew that she knew. "We will never be together again. Will we?"

Liam inched closer, hoping she would either submit to him and let him help her or pass out so he could rush her back to the house and call for help.

"You lied. You promised me, Liam. A long time ago and just now. You always lie. You're going to marry her." It came out like a prediction but was intended as a question.

Liam's silence answered her, and she bowed her weary head, then squeezed her eyes shut and sobbed.

"Ivy…" he went to console her, but she jerked her head to look at him.

"No!" She had a fire in her eyes now.

At this point, Liam knew the most important thing was getting the baby from her and getting him to the hospital. "Ivy, can I hold Barrett? Can I hold our son? Please?" He held out his hands.

"No, he's mine. You have Ben and Kimber. I want to keep this one." Her voice was different. It sounded nothing like her. She pressed the baby into her skin. His little nose disappeared into her flesh. Liam watched the baby's arms flail, and he tried to cry, but it was so muffled he could barely hear him.

"Ivy! Give me the baby!"

"He's sleepy, Liam. He needs to rest. Me and him need to rest together." She squeezed the baby harder and moved away from the tree and further into the darkness. The rain was falling again.

"Ivy, you're killing him. You're hurting him!"

And just like that, it was Liam who was mad. It was Liam who was on top of her. His hands were around her neck. Squeezing her skin with all his might. Her eyes looked into his. "It was always you, Ivy. You. You're the love of my life. Even after this night, I will always love you most." Spit spat out as he cried and bit down, not loosening the grip around her neck while she kicked and her hand squeezed his face. But no matter how far she dug her nails into his skin, he didn't stop. Finally, the look in her eyes changed back to the Ivy she was on the roof that summer night. She stopped fighting him. She stopped suffocating their new son. He was breathing and crying out. But Liam didn't loosen his grip around her neck and watched as the life left her eyes. He couldn't just kill the madness deep within her, so he'll have to bury all of her. Just as the darkness died, the same eyes of the woman who enjoyed dancing in the rain returned. He knew that she knew what he had to do as the skin on his hands burned against hers. Tears slid down her face as Liam's fell onto her chest. Suddenly the sun was bright, the air was warm, the sound of their children's laughter encircled them, and peace overcame Liam's heart as Ivy's stopped beating. Liam realized their life together began and ended in the rain.

Chapter Sixty

NOW

Later that night, after an ambulance sped away with Scar and his newborn son inside, he took a shovel into the forest, then dug a grave. He took one last look at Ivy before he lowered her into it. Most of Ivy was good, but parts of her were rotten. He had no choice but to end the continuous nightmare they had lived in and endured for far too long. The good died along with the bad. It had to be this way.

The truth was that Ivy had never taken anyone's life. But he had. He had tried to help her, but she was too far gone, and he understood that tonight, in the cold and dark forest. The Ivy he married all those years ago had passed away long before that night in the forest with Liam. But a judge would never see it that way. Justice didn't come from inside a courtroom with a jury but from his own two bare hands. And it would haunt him forever; he was sure of it.

But fear of her driving their children into a tree on a dark night, Ivy locking them inside a boat and removing the plug, or suffocating their new baby boy was irradicated when the air left her lungs for the last time. And Liam could live with that.

Never again would he and Scarlett search the faces of every single person they passed on the street. They would never be afraid of the dark again. In a way, Ivy was a monster under the bed. But that monster was put to rest now. He wanted to make sure that Ben, Kimber, and Barrett knew nothing of the creature that had hidden in the shadows but the mother who gave them life and loved them more than anything else in the whole world besides Liam.

Once Liam showered, he and the kids left for the hospital. He called Detective Karnes from his truck on the way. "I heard the doorbell, but by the time I reached the front door, a newborn baby was alone on the porch. I saw tail lights in the distance. I couldn't even make out the color of the car."

Scar had watched Liam take Ivy's life. She was still in shock when he arrived at the hospital. Once they were alone, Liam told her about the moment on the steps the night the kids went missing. "It was one time. I'm not even sure how it happened. It just did."

It had been a moment when he grasped onto anything he could to stay above water that day last summer. And at that moment, it was his ex-wife and the mother of his children. He told her he was sorry. And after a few days, she forgave him and became his wife.

Scarlett took to Barrett just as she had Ben and Kimber. Taking care of a family she didn't create wouldn't be easy. But she would finish it, and Liam knew she would do it well. He loved her even more for it. But the love in his heart for her would never compare to the love that didn't die along with Ivy in the woods that night. And it never would.

Epilogue

It's been five years since that night when Liam and Ivy ran into the woods, and only Liam walked out. On occasion, when the kids are at school, Scar is working or out running errands, and sometimes while they are all sleeping, Liam quietly goes out the back door. It's forty-nine steps to her. He counts every step every time he makes the short journey. He wonders if she can hear him coming. Not his footsteps, but his heart beating wildly inside his chest, excited to be close to her. His bare feet don't mind the cold grass, small pebbles, or even the scattered pine cones as he ventures into the woods. Twenty-four steps in, he can smell her. He steps over the dead fallen tree. It's at thirty-eight steps that he can hear her giggle, anticipating his arrival. He pushes the scratchy branches out of his way, picking up the pace. At forty-five steps, he is running and leaps over a small creek. At step forty-nine, there she is, like always, she's waiting for him. He stops. He lets the smell of vanilla invite him into the clearing where she stays. She's glowing, and happiness radiates from her as she reaches her sunkissed hand out to him. He moves closer to her and then lets her soft fingers rest in his hands. He takes her into his arms and holds her close. Sometimes he brings her long stem pale pink roses and leaves them where she sleeps. When they wilt and die, he brings her more. Sometimes he tells her things about the kids; other times, he sits quietly as they silently hold one another until he has to go. Today he doesn't want to let go. He lets the darkness fall, and beneath the moonlight, they dance to the sound of the night. Her long white, flowy dress sways, teasing the dirt beneath her bare feet. It's time for him to go. "Come with me." He whispers.

"I can't. You know that. I have to stay. I'll wait for you. I'll be right here when you come back."

Liam kisses her goodbye, but before he even opens his eyes, her presence is gone, and he's alone.

Once again, he walks the forty-nine steps back home, and he misses her. He savors the moments he gets to be with her. He loves that he hears her voice, smells her hair, and feels her warmth but never sees the madness. When he murdered her, that part turned black and seeped into the dirt. It went further down into the ground than where her bones rest. But sometimes, when Liam comes back home and crawls into bed next to Scar or makes a cup of coffee and drives to work, he wonders if a little of that madness stayed behind... with him. And if that's why he can still see her. But then he notices Kimber playing at the edge of the woods in the backyard near the pines. Her eyes glisten, and she smiles so big like she used to when she saw her mama. And then he knows that Ivy never left. She's still here.

Made in the USA
Middletown, DE
26 September 2023